'I want to make [illegible] Sam said.

AJ cocked her head t[illegible] what makes you think that will help you solve the case, Sherlock?'

'Elementary, my dear Watson,' he murmured, lowering his mouth to her neck. 'Haven't you ever come up with the solution to a particular problem when you weren't thinking about it at all?'

'Sure. All the time.' His mouth was now working magic on her shoulder and her skin felt hot and icy at the same time. She struggled to focus on the thread of their conversation. 'You think we'll figure out the solution if we have sex?'

Sam took the lobe of her ear between his teeth. 'Not sex, Ariana. I'm going to make love to you.'

'My name is AJ.'

'But you're Ariana, too. And making love is different than having sex. I'm going to show you.'

Please, she thought. 'Do you think Sherlock ever used this technique with Watson?'

Sam laughed, framing her face with his hands. 'God, I hope not. So, are you game?'

Wrapping her arms around him, she brought her mouth to his ear and tried a little magic of her own. 'I thought you'd never ask.'

Dear Reader,

The city is Manhattan, and the 'man-magnet' skirt is back in circulation! And AJ Potter has finally given in to the temptation to wear the infamous skirt. All she wants is to make the good old boys at her law firm take her seriously, but before she can even get to the office, she finds herself surrounded by men!

- a teenage delinquent who finds her 'hot'
- a retired jewel thief who thinks he's fallen in love with her
- a mugger who seems fixated on stealing her purse
- a sexy P.I. who is determined to convince her that one of her new clients just stole a five-million-dollar necklace from a museum

All PI Sam Romano wants to do is make sure his godfather doesn't go to jail. But every time he tries to talk to the old man, he runs smack into a little spitfire of an attorney. Each time he sees her, Sam becomes more convinced that the only way to get AJ Potter out of his way is to get her into his bed.

I hope you enjoy reading about AJ and Sam's romantic misadventures. And that you'll watch for the next instalment of the SINGLE IN THE CITY miniseries, when the skirt makes its way to San Francisco!

Enjoy,

Cara Summers

PS Come and visit me on the web at www.carasummers.com. And for more information about all the SINGLE IN THE CITY books, visit www.singleinthecity.org.

SHORT, SWEET AND SEXY

by

Cara Summers

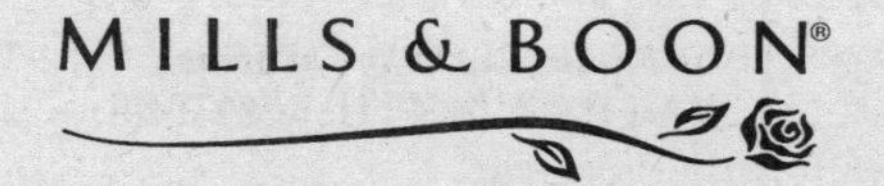

To my daughter-in-law, Mary Elizabeth Plante Hanlon.
In many ways, AJ Potter reminds me of you.
You're both smart, strong and loving. And you had
the courage to marry my son! I love you, Mary.

First published in Great Britain 2003
by Harlequin Mills & Boon Limited,
Eton House, 18-24 Paradise Road, Richmond, Surrey TW9 1SR

ISBN 0 263 83568 5

21-0803

Printed and bound in Spain
by Litografia Rosés S.A., Barcelona

Prologue

A. J. POTTER NEEDED A BREAK. As the taxi careened around a corner into Central Park, she threw out a hand to brace herself against the door and glanced down at the address she'd recorded in her Palm Pilot. She was not running away. All she was going to do was move into an apartment, not ten blocks away from her aunt and uncle's.

In comparison, it wasn't considered running away when you asked a judge for a postponement in court.

And that's all she needed—a postponement from her family, a little vacation from her Uncle Jamison and her cousin Rodney who sat at the dinner table every night, talking about the cases Rodney was being assigned at the law firm and she wasn't. Most of all she needed a reprieve from her Aunt Margery whose mission in life was to match her up with a man who wouldn't bring disgrace on the Potter family name. If she had to endure another date with one more Mr. Perfect handpicked by her aunt, she was going to...do just what she *was* doing. Move out!

Leaning back, A.J. closed her eyes as the taxi wound its way through Central Park. Somehow in the seven years she'd spent away at college and then in law school, she'd forgotten what a misfit she was in the Potter family. But living with them for the past year had certainly refreshed her memory. Worse than that, it was beginning to undermine her confidence. Ever since Uncle Jamison and Aunt Margery had taken her in at the age of seven, she'd tried—and failed—to prove to them that she could be a *Potter,* that she wasn't at all like her mother.

A.J.'s eyes snapped open the minute the taxi lurched to the curb.

"The Willoughby," the driver said.

After paying the fare and stepping out onto the sidewalk, A.J. studied the building. It was small with the same kind of understated elegance that characterized her aunt and uncle's building. She sighed. Her aunt would definitely approve.

The real estate agent who'd given her the tip about the apartment had hinted at something different. Pushing down her disappointment, A.J. slipped her Palm Pilot into her purse and strode toward the door of the Willoughby.

The moment she stepped inside, she stopped short. The scene in front of her was definitely a tad unusual—even for New York. The fact that it was taking place in the lobby of a Central Park West apartment building had her thinking that she'd tumbled down a rabbit hole into Alice's Wonderland.

The woman with the wavy brown hair appeared normal enough. The suitcases and slightly out-of-style clothes, as well as the confused expression on her face, pegged her as a visitor to the Big Apple.

The man was an entirely different matter. He was wearing a baggy blue polka-dot bathing suit and standing in the middle of a small wading pool decorated with cartoon fish. Sun poured down from a skylight, turning the zinc oxide he'd smeared across his nose a bright shade of lime green. "Surfin' USA" blared out of the boom box beside his striped deck chair.

A.J. smiled slowly. If she wanted a reprieve from the stuffiness of her aunt and uncle's condominium and from being a *Potter* twenty-four hours a day, she couldn't have picked a better place. She was definitely going to take this apartment.

"Password!" the man with the green nose shouted above the pounding rhythm of the Beach Boys.

The woman with the suitcases shook her head.

A.J. moved forward.

"I'm waaaaiiiiiting." He sang this time instead of shouting.

Nice voice, A.J. noted, and now that she was closer, she recognized the tattoo on his left forearm. The moment the Beach Boys faded, she said, "Toto."

"Close but no cigar," he said and then sang the opening stanza of "Somewhere Over the Rainbow." "Are you here for the apartment?"

"Yes." A.J. found herself speaking in unison with the suitcase woman.

"You and about forty others," he said, peering at them over his sunglasses. "Tavish Mclain is the man you'll have to convince, and this is his day of glory—the day he dreams of the other 364 days of the year. He is surrounded by women, and each one of them is willing to do whatever it takes to get his apartment."

"We'd like to join them," A.J. said. The real estate agent had warned her that there would be an auction, and she needed to size up her opponents.

He glanced quickly around, then leaned closer and spoke in a stage whisper. "You might try naming the actor who played the cowardly lion."

"Bert Lahr." A.J. and the suitcase woman spoke again at the same time.

A grin split his face. "Excellent."

"Bert Lahr is the password, then?" A.J. asked.

"No. But I like the fact that you're *Wizard of Oz* movie buffs, so you may pass."

"Thanks," A.J. said as she hurried toward the elevator.

Oh, this was getting better and better. She definitely wasn't in Kansas anymore.

"The name's Franco," the man with the green nose called after them. "Franco Rossi. You're going to see it in lights someday."

A.J. pressed the elevator button and when the door slid open, she helped the suitcase woman muscle the biggest one in.

"Thanks. I'm Claire Dellafield," the woman said.

"A. J. Potter." She looked the woman up and down. "I guess we're competitors."

Claire nodded. "Do you think the apartment's going to be expensive? If so, I don't have enough money to be much competition."

A.J. thought the apartment might be very expensive. She'd heard about it through a broker for whom she'd done a closing that morning. Tavish Mclain, an eccentric and thrifty Scot, had money to burn and just couldn't miss an opportunity to make more. Rather than allow his apartment to sit empty for three months while he went off on holiday, he ran what the broker had described to her as a sort of auction-lottery to rent it for the summer. The moment she'd heard that it was a rental and that she could move in immediately, A.J. had taken it as a sign. And the fact that the address was Central Park West would stifle some of her family's concern.

When her mother had left the family home she'd moved to a coldwater flat in the Village with the man who'd become A.J.'s father.

A.J. would never do that to her family. The address of the Willoughby would definitely reassure her aunt and uncle of that. And the money wouldn't be a problem for her because of the trust fund her mother had left her. But Claire Dellafield looked as though it might be a problem for her. She also looked beat and a little lost. Manhattan could be a tough city for the uninitiated, and A.J.'s heart went out to her. "Want to join forces and bid together?"

"I don't know. I—"

A.J. nodded as the door slid open. "Smart girl. Someone warned you about the big bad city." Unzipping her purse, she pulled out a card. "I have a hunch that the bidding might be brutal and I intend to win. Think about it."

The noise was coming from the apartment at the end of the hall, and dozens of people were jammed around the door of 6C. At barely five feet tall, she couldn't see over them, so she wiggled and elbowed her way through. Reaching the door and finding Claire right behind her, A.J. helped her heave the suitcases into the foyer.

The room was packed with women, mostly blondes in various shapes and sizes. They ranged in age from…A.J. figured the one in the latex capris and midriff-baring tank top to be about twenty, and the one just entering with the bouffant hair and the poodle had to be in her seventies. That poodle lady might have money, she decided. The huge rock on her right hand looked very real.

Eyes narrowed, A.J. rose to her toes and peered around shoulders to scan the room again. She caught glimpses of a tacky Southwestern decor. Could that have been a longhorn cow over the fireplace? It was only by leaping up that she finally spotted the broker who'd tipped her off to the auction. Roger Whitfield, who was handling the sublet for Tavish, stood on the steps leading up to the loft.

When she landed back on her feet, her eyes collided briefly with a tall woman—not a blonde—who carried a package under her arm and had a determined look on her face. Very determined. Well, A.J. was determined too.

Someone waved a check high over her head. "Here it is, folks. Good faith money. Forty-five hundred dollars—three months—up front."

"Hey!" someone shouted.

"That's not fair!"

"I can't go that high!"

"Tavish promised to rent this place to me for eight hundred."

As pandemonium broke loose around her, A.J. pulled out her checkbook and cell phone. Women surged around her in waves, some heading toward the stairs, others toward the door. The tall brunette with the package was pushed up next to Claire's biggest suitcase.

"This is ridiculous." Tapping her foot, A.J. punched numbers into the cell phone, and waited. After counting ten rings, she decided that Roger, now besieged by blond ambition, was not going to take her call. Finally, she turned to the two women beside her. She'd overheard enough of their conversation to understand that the brunette had just offered Claire a free room at the hotel she worked at.

"Why would you do that?" Claire asked. "You don't even know me."

"Because I can. Because helping the sisterhood was something my mother drilled into me. And, hey, I get off on warm fuzzy feelings in my tummy."

A.J. smiled. She was beginning to like the tall determined woman with the box. "So do I, but they don't always come from giving away freebie hotel rooms."

The woman returned her smile. "Samantha Baldwin."

A.J. shook the offered hand. "A. J. Potter. You sounded a little like a madam gathering a poor waif into her house of ill repute. I already made the same first great impression on her. I think we scared her."

"I'm not scared," said Claire. "Just fascinated by abnormal human behavior. Abnormal for a New Yorker, that is."

Making a sudden decision, A.J. pulled out her Palm Pilot and checked on the information Roger, the broker, had given her. Then she turned her attention back to the two women. "According to my information, this place has three bedrooms."

"I don't smoke. I can do eighteen hundred a month, but I don't want to."

A.J. couldn't help but admire Samantha's quick uptake and no-nonsense style. "Nonsmoker. I'm in for two grand."

"You'd get the big bedroom then."

Perfectly in sync, they both looked at Claire.

"What's your name?" A.J. asked.

"Claire Dellafield. Why?"

"Get with the program," Samantha said. "We're forming a rental coalition. You want in?"

Claire stood. "You mean we'd room together?"

"Mental functions seem to be intact," said A.J. "Do you smoke?"

Claire shook her head. "But I can learn."

Samantha laughed. "She's in for the entertainment value alone."

A.J. nodded her agreement. Plus, she guessed Claire needed this apartment as much as they did. "How much can you contribute to the rent?"

Claire drew in a deep breath. "Eight hundred."

"That's forty-six hundred. Surely the rent won't go any higher," A.J. said.

Just then, the door to the apartment swung open and two men entered.

"Tavish!" several blondes squealed as they ran towards him, arms outstretched.

"Let this play out," A.J. suggested. Getting a handle on the opposition always paid off in the courtroom.

Samantha and Claire took her advice, but it wasn't a pretty sight. The women were fawning all over the man in a sage-green faux leather vest—with fringe. A.J. knew the type well.

He might dress a little less conservatively, but Tavish Mclain reminded her of all the rich, middle-aged, self-absorbed Mr. Perfects that her aunt had been setting her up with for the past year.

The dates from hell were one of her prime motivations for getting out of her aunt and uncle's home. Aunt Margery's mission was to marry her off before she disgraced the family the way her mother had. With that whole scenario off her plate, she figured she could concentrate all her attention on making her uncle take her more seriously at the law firm. For the past year, her assignments at Hancock, Potter and King had consisted of real estate closings and research. She was the only Potter woman to join the firm since it had been founded, and she definitely didn't fit into the good old boy network.

But she was going to. And if she could prove herself at the law firm, maybe her aunt and uncle would stop worrying that she would follow in her mother's footsteps and they would finally accept her.

She needed this apartment. But as she rose once more to her toes and saw the bevy of blondes waving checks in Tavish's face, she feared the odds of getting it were slipping away. She remembered what Franco Rossi had said about this being the day Tavish Mclain lived the other 364 days for. She could see why. One woman was literally pawing his vest.

A.J. glanced at her two companions. No, they were definitely not the pawing types—which was why she liked them.

Hmmmm. Tapping her foot, she was desperately searching her mind for a different approach when Samantha said, "Stand in front of me."

A.J. watched her tear the brown paper off the package she was holding.

"What are you doing?" Claire asked.

"I've got something in here that may convince Mr. Mclain to give us anything we want."

"What?" A.J. asked. "A gun?"

"Even better," Samantha replied, pulling out a wad of silky, black fabric. "A magic skirt."

A.J. exchanged a skeptical glance with Claire. Then Claire cleared her throat. "Did you say a *magic* skirt?"

"I know it sounds crazy," Samantha said as she shook out wrinkles, then began to pull it on over the skirt she was wearing. "But it's a regular man-magnet. According to the legend, it's woven out of a special fiber that will make men do anything for the woman who wears it. It's even supposed to have the power to bring your true love to you...yada, yada, yada."

"You're kidding, right?" A.J. watched her shimmy out of the old skirt underneath. The "magic" garment was simple, black, basic. She could have sworn she had one just like it in her closet. She'd bought it at Bloomingdale's right after Christmas. A quick look around told her that the only one paying any attention to Samantha's quick change routine was the elderly lady with the poodle and the rock.

"Look, I don't believe it either, but it can't hurt," Samantha said to A.J.

A.J. had to agree with her on that. Jumping up, she glimpsed a blonde with black lipstick, pulling out her pen, ready to sign on the dotted line.

"Follow me, ladies," Samantha said. Then, leading the way, she cut a path through the sea of blondes toward the man in the fringed green vest.

A.J. looked at Claire and shrugged. "What can it hurt?"

"True," Claire said. "And if it doesn't work, we can always resort to Plan B."

"What Plan B?" A.J. asked.

"We can hang Tavish out the window by his ankles until he agrees to sublet his apartment to us."

A.J. grinned. "A regular win-win situation." Then she turned her attention to Samantha as she advanced slowly on Tavish Mclain. With each step, she wiggled her hips. A.J. could have sworn the skirt caught the light and glimmered.

"I'm Samantha Baldwin." One last step and wiggle brought Samantha within an arm's length of the man in the green fringed vest.

"Tavish Mclain," he said as he grasped her extended hand.

"You have the perfect apartment," Samantha said, beaming a smile at him.

"I call...it...home," Tavish stuttered as he pumped her hand.

For a moment neither of them said a thing. They just stood there, hands clasped and staring at each other.

"I'd like to call it home, too, for the summer," Samantha finally said.

"Well, I... Well, I'm sure—" Tavish began.

Then Roger Whitfield and another broker crowded forward, introducing themselves, but Tavish didn't relinquish Samantha's hand.

Eyes narrowed, A.J. took a minute to size up the situation. The three men had their eyes locked on Samantha. Even the other women were beginning to notice it.

The blonde in black lipstick waved her check. "Just a minute. I've given you a check for forty-five hundred."

"Roger, give Meredith back her check," Tavish murmured, never taking his eyes off Samantha.

"So I'll give you another for six thousand," the blonde said.

Quickly, A.J. scribbled out a check and tucked it in Samantha's free hand. Two thousand for the first month would match the blonde's offer.

"Here you go..." Samantha glanced at A.J.'s check. "Two thousand dollars."

Tavish smiled. "So you did want to pay all the rent up front after all?"

All the rent? A.J. glanced at the skirt. Had they just rented a Central Park West apartment for the summer for two thousand dollars?

Tavish stuck the check in his vest pocket. "The perfect tenant, wouldn't you say, Roger?"

"I'd...say...so."

A.J. tore her eyes from the skirt to check out the broker. Any minute now, Roger was going to drool. The other broker was doing that already. It was time to make her move. "Gentlemen, which one of you has the papers we should sign?" She was pretty sure it was Roger, but at the moment she'd settle for someone who wasn't catatonic.

"Papers?" Roger asked.

A.J. snapped her fingers in front of his face. "An indemnity clause? Terms of lease? Liability release?"

To her relief, Roger blinked, then fumbled in his pocket for papers. Ruthlessly, A.J. pulled him aside, and made him focus on the lease agreement. Out of the corner of her eye, she saw Claire take the other broker by the arm. "You and I are on crowd control. Thanks for coming, everybody."

The only ones in the room who hadn't moved were Samantha and Tavish. They were still gripping hands, still staring into each other's eyes. But Samantha seemed to be perfectly all right as she explained to Tavish that she had two roommates. A.J. glanced once more at the skirt before she focused her entire attention on the lease agreement.

"It's standard, although I should probably mention Cleo,"

Roger said, his gaze drifting back to Samantha. "Could you introduce me?"

"To Cleo?" A.J. asked.

"No," Roger said, gesturing vaguely toward the woman with the bouffant hair and the rock on her hand. "Cleo's the poodle, lives in 6B. You're expected to walk her. It's part of Tavish's arrangement with his neighbors."

"No problem," A.J. said. She'd see to it that it wasn't. She wanted signatures on the bottom line before Tavish Mclain could come out of his skirt trance and change his mind.

And she got them! An hour later when A.J. stepped out into the bright sunlight on Central Park West, she gave a little jump of pure pleasure. Not only did she have a new place to live, but she had two new roommates—women she'd seemed to click with immediately. She hugged the knowledge to her.

Not bad for the day that she'd chosen to build a new life for herself.

And then there was the skirt. Samantha had put it in her bedroom closet before she'd taken off for work. If A.J. hadn't seen it, she never would have believed it.

There was definitely something about that skirt—something that might come in handy if she couldn't solve the problem of being taken seriously at Hancock, Potter and King by herself.

Pushing the thought out of her mind, A.J. strode toward the corner. She preferred solving things by herself.

1

SHE WAS LATE.

The fact that the pretty, petite and very punctual blonde had not burst through the door of her apartment building at seven-fifteen sharp had Sam Romano's fingers tingling, and that was a sign that something bad was about to go down. In his ten years as a P.I., his fingers had never failed him.

Nerves. He couldn't afford them now. Nor could he afford to be thinking about that tiny little blonde with the initials A.J.P. embossed on her handbag. She had nothing to do with the case he was supposed to be focusing on.

Rubbing his hands on his threadbare jeans, Sam shifted his gaze to the Grenelle Museum across the street. He'd had it staked out for five days, ever since the Abelard necklace had gone on display. The museum had hired Sterling Security, the firm he worked for, because they'd wanted to take some extra precautions with a five million-dollar necklace on display.

They'd made a wise decision. Sam knew from the two assistants he'd stationed at the side and back of the building that someone had climbed up the back of the building at 6:30 a.m.

What he hadn't known until he'd seen for himself was that the man was none other than his godfather, Pierre Rabaut, a prominent New York jazz club owner and retired jewel thief. Sam had gotten a good glimpse of Pierre through his binoculars just before he'd seen the thin, wiry man disappear through the skylight at six-thirty-five.

That had been forty minutes ago. The museum's alarms would be turned off at seven-thirty to allow for a shift change in the security staff, and Sam was banking on the fact that Pierre would choose that moment to make his escape through the front doors.

Always do the unexpected.

It was one of the mottoes that Pierre Rabaut lived by. And because he had shared that piece of advice and more with the youngest son of an old friend, Pierre Rabaut was going to be caught with the Abelard necklace in his possession...but he was not going to be arrested. Sam wasn't going to allow that to happen.

For the first time in his life, he was about to betray a client to save an old friend. Pierre Rabaut had been like a second father to him, especially during the days after his mother had died and then again later when his father had met and fallen in love with Isabelle Sheridan, a woman who hadn't been willing to become a part of his father's life. Pierre had always been there for him, and Sam was going to see that he didn't go to jail.

If a job is worth doing, it is worth doing well.

Sam's lips twisted wryly. That piece of advice had come from Pierre, too. But this was the first time that doing his job well had put him between a rock and a hard place. He'd been hired to make sure the Abelard necklace wasn't stolen. He intended to do just that. But making sure that Pierre Rabaut wasn't arrested—that might cost him his job.

Flexing his fingers to ease a fresh wave of tingles, Sam stifled the urge to glance at his watch. His disguise as one of New York City's homeless would be worthless if Pierre happened to glance out of one of the museum's windows and catch him checking the time.

Instead, Sam shifted his gaze down 75th Street. Two taxis, horns blaring, squeezed their way through the intersection. Halfway down the block a delivery man dropped a case of soft drinks on the cement and then let out a stream of curses. Over them, Sam caught a snatch of lyrics from a rap song pouring out of the open window of a pickup truck double-parked across the street.

And there was still no sign of the tiny blonde.

Not that he should be even thinking about her. He needed to keep all of his attention focused on Pierre. But for the life of him he hadn't been able to get the woman out of his head. She just didn't...fit.

He could recall in great detail that first time he'd seen her walking toward him. He'd pegged her for a rich socialite—the kind of woman he always steered clear of. Still, she'd been worth a second glance and the stakeout was proving to be long and boring. A nice fantasy always made the time go faster. So he'd begun to indulge in one.

The easy way she'd swung her briefcase had told him she worked out regularly in a gym. He'd pictured that compact little body of hers in designer workout clothes that clung to every curve, her fair skin slick with sweat. He hadn't a doubt in the world that she would attack each and every piece of equipment in the gym, one by one, with the same energy and concentration that she exuded when she left her building and headed toward the subway each morning.

Would she make love with that same intensity and passion? The question had barely slipped into his mind when she'd stopped and tucked a twenty-dollar bill into his cup. Startled, he'd glanced up and met her eyes, and for one moment he could have sworn his mind had gone blank. By the time he'd recovered, she'd been halfway down the block, and he'd nearly gotten up and gone after her. Sam shook his head at the memory. He'd nearly blown his cover and gone running down the street after her! No one—man or woman—had ever made him forget he was on a job.

The second day she'd stopped, he'd had his wits about him until she'd surprised him again by speaking to him. She'd asked him if he was interested in getting a job. When he'd said yes—hell, he'd felt compelled to when he was staring into those eyes of hers—she said she'd look into it. Then she'd dropped another twenty into his cup. Thoroughly bemused, he'd gazed after her wondering if she were some kind of blonde, violet-eyed guardian angel sent down from on high to look after the homeless.

The last two days had followed the same pattern. She'd stop, tuck money into his cup and give him little updates on how her job search was going.

Sam frowned as he switched his gaze back to the museum doors. He just couldn't figure her out. Rich socialites didn't stop to chat with homeless people, and they certainly didn't try to find jobs for them.

"Any sign of movement, Mr. Romano?"

Luis Santos's voice, carrying clearly through the wireless device in his ear, had Sam ruthlessly reining in his thoughts and focusing on the museum. He had two young men, Luis and Tyrone Bass, stationed at the back and side doors of the building Pierre had entered. Luis and Tyrone were P.I.s in training, or so he'd told the judge when he'd arranged to supervise the community service they'd been sentenced to. He hadn't told either of them yet what he intended to do today.

If he did it right, he would never have to tell them. But the timing had to be perfect.

"Everything's quiet here," he said. Except for the rap song, he thought as he glanced at the pickup truck. The driver was reading the morning paper and sipping coffee, seemingly oblivious to the racket his radio was making.

Once more Sam flexed his fingers to ease the tingling. "You got the time?"

"Seven-twenty," Luis said. "He's been in there fifty minutes."

"He'll be walking out the front door in ten," Sam predicted.

He didn't have a doubt in the world that his godfather was going to walk out the museum door with the Abelard necklace. He'd researched the man thoroughly when he was a kid, and there'd been no jewel thief in Europe to match him when he'd decided to retire forty years ago.

The problem would be to convince his godfather to put the necklace back before anyone knew it was missing. It was a task that required his full attention. He certainly didn't have time to think about the tiny blond woman who wanted to save him from a life on the streets.

"LET'S JUST SEE," A.J. said as she slipped the skirt over her head and pulled it down. Then she studied her reflection in the mirror. What it looked like was any other black skirt. She had one she'd bought from Bloomingdale's hanging in her closet just like it. Almost. The thing was—this one might look like the other one, but it felt...silky...and light...almost as if she wasn't wearing anything at all. And it fit perfectly.

If it had been too big or too tight, she would have had an excuse to call the whole experiment off. "It feels sort of—different."

"Isn't that the whole point?" Samantha handed her one of the three mugs of coffee she was juggling. "If you're going to get the men at your law firm to start thinking of you as something other than a research nerd, changing your dress style is an excellent first step."

"The skirt shows off your legs much better than those slacks you always wear," Claire pointed out.

A.J. studied herself in the mirror. She wore slacks and jackets because in a law firm that had only a few token women on its roster, she felt she fit in better. Behind her, she could see her two roommates studying her as closely as she was studying herself. It was hard to believe that she'd known Samantha Baldwin and Claire Dellafield for less than two months. In the short amount of time since they'd rented Tavish Mclain's apartment, she'd begun to feel as if she'd known them forever. She shifted her attention back to the skirt. "Don't you think it's a little short?"

"It's much shorter on me. I was thinking you could tape up the hem a little. All the better to wow those stuffed shirts with," Samantha said with a wicked grin.

"I think it's fine," Claire said.

"I don't know. I just don't feel quite myself in it."

"That's perfectly normal," Claire said. "You put on a skirt that's supposed to have the power to draw your true love to you—that's a scary step."

A.J. held up a hand. "Time out. I'm not looking for my true love. All I want is to be taken seriously at work and for Uncle Jamison to trust me enough to assign me to a litigation case. The pro bono cases I've been doing don't seem to carry any weight with the executive board." Her dream was to become a partner at Hancock, Potter and King. Once she did that, surely her aunt and uncle would stop worrying that she was going to blemish the Potter name by running away with a ne'er-do-well like her mother had.

Claire exchanged a glance with Samantha, then said, "It's a little hard to predict exactly what will happen when you wear it. The skirt has a tendency to surprise you."

That was one of the reasons A.J. had waited nearly two months to give the skirt a whirl. And first, she'd done some research. The simple black skirt that had helped them rent Tavish Mclain's apartment already had quite a history in

Manhattan. She'd found the three articles that had appeared in *Metropolitan* magazine, all giving evidence to the skirt's power to attract men. It had even made the news on a morning talk show, and a smart entrepreneur had sold a department store chain a whole line of knockoffs.

But the skirt A.J. was wearing was the real McCoy. Samantha's cousin, Kate Talavera-Logan, had mailed it to her right after her wedding. And both Claire and Samantha had testified to the fact that the incident that had gotten them the apartment had not been an isolated one. The skirt did have some kind of power over men.

"Too late for second thoughts," Samantha said glancing at her watch. "You're already running late."

"Besides, what have you got to lose?" Claire asked. "Even if you strike out at the office, you'll probably get a date with a tall, dark and handsome stranger."

"I'll pass on the date," A.J. said. "The only tall, dark and handsome stranger I've seen lately is the homeless man camped around the corner of 75th Street. And I'm certainly not going to date him." She bit down hard on her tongue before she told them that she was trying to get the homeless man a job. They would think she was nuts. And how could she explain why? It had to do with his eyes—and that intent, searching look he'd given her the first time their eyes had met. She could still recall the strange sense of recognition that she'd experienced. "I'd really be in a pickle if he turned out to be my true love."

She'd be just like her mother then—falling in love with the wrong kind of man. To push the uncomfortable thought out of her mind, she raised her coffee mug. "I propose a toast. To the power of the skirt." She clinked mugs with her roommates and was about to take a drink of her coffee when she saw a flash of light in the mirror. "What was that?"

"What was what?" Claire asked.

"I saw something. I think the skirt flashed," A.J. said.

"Nerves." Claire put a hand on her shoulder. "I felt a little apprehensive the first time I wore the skirt too. But you'll get used to it."

"Eventually you might even get used to the strange way that men react to it," Samantha added.

A.J. studied her friends' faces in the mirror. Their faint smiles told her that they were slipping off into their own private worlds again. They'd been doing that more and more lately, and it had all started when they had each first worn the skirt. It was beginning to make her feel like an outsider. The moment the thought drifted into her mind, she stiffened her shoulders. That was not going to happen. Living with Samantha and Claire for the past two months, she'd felt as if she'd belonged for the first time since her parents had died. She liked it. And she wanted to feel that way at the law firm too. "Okay, I'm off to give this thing a little test drive at the office."

"Good luck," Claire said, taking her mug.

"You go girl," Samantha said, handing A.J. her purse.

A.J. was smiling when Claire and Samantha pushed her out into the hall and closed the door behind her. How different her life had become since she moved into this apartment. She had never felt this at home growing up in her uncle and aunt's place.

"Yoo hoo! Ms. Potter, how fortuitous that we should run into each other. I was just going to knock on your door."

A.J. bit back a sigh. Of course, every silver lining had its cloud. And Mrs. Higgenbotham and her French poodle Cleo were a huge gray one that daily threatened to rain on apartment 6C's parade. The three-month rental of 6C came with a catch—an expectation—as Roger the broker had explained to them. And what it boiled down to was the care of Cleo, a prize-winning show dog. Strictly speaking, sublets were illegal in the building, but regular tenants looked the other way and never breathed a word of it to Marlon, the owner, as long as certain "neighborly favors" were exchanged. A.J. could only thank her lucky stars that it was Claire's turn to walk Cleo in the park on Thursdays.

A.J. turned to give Mrs. Higgenbotham a smile and blinked at the peach cloud filling the hallway. In two months she should have grown used to the older woman's appearance, but then she was never quite sure what color the hair would be. Today it was definitely peach, a perfect match to the billowing caftan that seemed to be in perpetual motion around her.

"Cleo isn't eating again. I've decided she needs an emergency therapy session. Dr. Fielding is opening up his office early to fit her in. Isn't that wonderful of him?"

Several more appropriate adjectives ran through A.J.'s mind—greedy and opportunistic heading the list—but she kept them to herself as she began to edge her way backwards toward the elevator. She didn't need a Ph.D. in pet therapy to recognize that Cleo's problem was that she was lonely. She wanted a mate. Most of the male dogs that she met on her daily walks in the park could testify to that in court. The problem was that Mrs. H. was determined to mate Cleo with another pedigreed poodle, and Cleo preferred commoners.

Mrs. Higgenbotham and the peach cloud wafted toward her. "I have a favor to ask. Could you possibly drop Cleo off? I'm not dressed to go out, and Dr. Fielding wants her at 7:45. Miss Dellafield isn't scheduled to take her on her walk until this afternoon. You don't have to wait for her. I can pick her up myself. Or…" she paused to glance back at the door of 6C, "or I can make other arrangements."

A.J. took the leash from Mrs. Higgenbotham's outstretched hand. "No problem." Experience had taught her the hard way that agreeing to the woman's requests was the quickest way out of the apartment building.

"Bless you." Mrs. Higgenbotham pressed a card into her hand. "Dr. Fielding's office is on Park Avenue. I'll wave goodbye to Cleo from my living room window."

In the safety of the elevator, A.J. glanced at her watch. Seven twenty-five. She was ten minutes behind schedule and delivering Cleo to Dr. Fielding would delay her even further. And there was still Franco Rossi to deal with. Hopefully, she could slip past him before he could notice she was wearing the skirt.

All hope of accomplishing that vaporized when the doors slid open and she found herself staring at the doorman.

"Thank heavens," Franco said, sweeping a hand to his chest and fluttering a small Japanese fan with the other. "I was worried. You're ten minutes late!"

"Mrs. H. stopped me," A.J. explained as Cleo yipped at Franco and then, head down, dashed for the door. For some reason, Franco seemed to be the one male that Cleo had no use for. A.J. picked up her pace.

The door to the building was less than ten yards away, but, thanks to Franco, her best personal time for crossing the lobby was five minutes. And that was only if she kept her sentences short, avoided asking questions, and didn't comment on anything he was wearing—like the kimono in shades of red, pink and vermilion. The colors were bright enough to make her eyes water. And she was sure, though she'd only risked a glance, that the clogs he wore added a good three inches to his height.

"They're doing a musical version of *Teahouse of the August Moon* off Broadway," Franco explained. "What do you think?"

Since she really didn't want to think anything about it, A.J. said, "Cleo has stopped eating."

"Poor thing," Franco said.

Cleo yipped again.

Five yards short of the glass doors, A.J. halted and broke one of her rules. "What do you know about Dr. Fielding?"

Franco's brows shot up. "He's a very successful pet therapist—works a side specialty putting his clients through past-life regressions. Charges a bundle for it."

She took another step toward the door, then stopped. "Cleo doesn't need a past life regression. She's young, she's lonely and she's healthy. What she needs is a man."

"Don't we all?" Franco asked in a heartfelt tone.

A.J. blinked. No, she wasn't talking about herself. Her problem was she had too many men in her life. She didn't need any more. She was definitely talking about Cleo. "What good does it do her to win top prizes at the Westminster Kennel Show if she's lonely and she can't eat—and worse still, she can't even play with the other dogs in the park? She's doomed to be lonely until Mrs. H. locates the perfect pedigreed poodle for her."

"Honey, she's doomed to be lonely forever if she keeps attacking them. How's the lawsuit going?"

"You know I can't talk about it," A.J. said. No one at the firm was going to let her forget the fact that the first lawsuit she brought to Hancock, Potter and King was a dog-bite case.

"I heard tell that the other poodle had to have eight stitches and they're suing for millions in pain and suffering."

Too late, A.J. realized that Franco's gaze was moving over her in a slow, careful assessment. Was he going to recognize the skirt? He'd been after her to wear it, and she'd sworn to him that she never would.

"Nice blazer," he said. "That shade of lemon yellow looks great on you. I was right. Your colors are definitely light spring. Most definitely."

When his gaze moved lower to her shoes, she let out the breath she'd been holding. Maybe he wouldn't notice.

Fat chance, she thought. Franco noticed *everything*. On top of that, he was a man, and, according to Samantha and Claire, men noticed things about the skirt that women were oblivious to. She began to inch her way backward toward the door.

Suddenly, Franco lunged past her, teetering on the three-inch-high clogs, and threw himself against the plate-glass door to block her exit.

"You're wearing it. I knew you would. You almost had me fooled there for a minute. I actually thought you were talking about Cleo—but you're talking about yourself. You're actually going to see if you can reel in a man with that skirt. And you owe me an Alexander Hamilton. I told you that sooner or later, you'd succumb to the power of the skirt. Hand it over!"

Calmly, she reached into her purse, pulled a ten-dollar bill from her wallet, and placed it in Franco's outstretched palm.

Quick as a blink, he pressed it to his lips and then shoved it in the pocket of his kimono. Finally, he fastened his eyes once more on the skirt as he minced around her in a slow circle. "Very nice."

Cleo yipped again.

Franco fixed her with a look. "Settle down, girl. I'm not one of your stud poodles. My hands are registered lethal weapons."

"How can you tell it's *the* skirt?" A.J. asked. Then a disturbing thought struck her. "You're not...starting to..." How was she going to put it? "You're not starting to have any special feelings for me or anything?"

Startled, Franco stopped in his tracks and stared at her. "Perish the thought. I've already found my true love." He winked at her. "And Marlon wasn't wearing a skirt."

"I'm sorry. I'm just a little nervous."

Franco patted her arm. "That's perfectly natural. I remember exactly what it was like to be single and alone in New York. Terrible. It's a dating wasteland out there, and any little thing that will help is a blessing. I remember those singles' bars were right out of a horror movie. And you know how I feel about them."

Everyone knew how Franco felt about horror movies and just about everything else. His favorite movie was *The Wizard of Oz.* He hated Chinese food, loved sushi, preferred his opera sung in the original language and subtitled, hated free rock concerts in Central Park but had no objection to free Shakespeare because those performances were less crowded. And, above all, he loved living in New York.

It occurred to A.J. that there wasn't much she didn't know about Franco since he was bound and determined to share all aspects of his life with anyone who lived in the building—even on a summer sublet. And he had a knack for prying as much information out of the tenants as he imparted to them.

Stepping back, he glanced at the skirt again. "But you won't have any trouble attracting men while you're wearing that little number."

"I don't want to attract them—at least, not the way you mean. I just want to *influence* them. At eight-thirty this morning, we have our monthly department meeting at Hancock, Potter and King. Trial cases will be assigned, and while I would have preferred to get one on my own merits, I've decided that desperate measures are called for."

Franco grinned from ear to ear. "I'd say you have a good shot. When you stand in the doorway with the light behind you, that skirt becomes almost transparent."

"Transparent?"

"A woman with legs like yours shouldn't have any trouble

influencing men." Opening the door, Franco gave her a little shove into the street.

"You and Cleo should make quite a team."

As the door swung shut behind her, A.J. drew in a deep breath and let it out. As much as she might dread it, the gauntlet she had to run each morning to make it out the door was good training for the job facing her at her uncle's law firm. Today was the day, she promised herself as she charged up the street with Cleo in tow. By five o'clock tonight she was going to have a client, and she would be on her way to court.

Cleo's sad little whine had A.J. automatically tightening her grip on the leash and glancing across the street. A St. Bernard had pulled his owner to a dead stop and the dog was straining at his leash to cross the street.

Quickly, she tightened her grip on Cleo's leash. "I know you'd rather go play, sweetie. But we don't have time this morning."

Drawing in another deep breath, she strode toward the corner. The one thing that she hadn't shared with Franco, or either of her roommates, was that if Uncle Jamison did not assign her to a trial case today, she was going to have to think about resigning from the firm. It was the last thing in the world she wanted to do.

EVEN THOUGH HE HAD his eyes on Pierre Rabaut walking down the steps of the museum, Sam knew the moment that the little blonde and the poodle stepped onto the sidewalk and started toward him. The tingling in his fingers immediately intensified.

Her timing couldn't have been worse. Unless Sam missed his guess, Pierre would step into the street just about the time that A.J.P. would be slipping a bill into his cup and giving him an update on her job search. The last thing he wanted right now was to be distracted.

Quickly, he scanned the street, taking in the double-parked pickup truck with the driver who loved rap songs and a car that had just pulled into the curb farther up the block. A man, medium height, thin, with a beard, rounded the corner on Pierre's side of the street. Other than that, he and the blonde and the dog were the only others in sight.

He had to wait to make his move. He couldn't allow Pierre any possibility of escaping. If he were going to save his godfather from going to jail, he had to get him to replace the necklace immediately—before anyone knew it was gone.

The mistake he made was in glancing at the blonde. The moment he did, he felt his mind empty and his stomach tighten as if he'd just sustained a swift, hard blow.

He was deadly certain that he'd never seen legs quite that…for the life of him, he couldn't find a word to describe them. He could only stare at her as she moved toward him with that quick, sure stride.

The skirt—what there was of it—clung to her hips and thighs like a second skin. Except that skin wasn't transparent. Or was he merely fantasizing the thigh-high stockings trimmed with a band of lace?

"Good morning." She swung her purse off her shoulder and reached into it at the same moment that a motor revved loudly and the poodle began to bark. Sam tore his gaze from the woman to Pierre, but, even then, it took a moment for the scene in front of him to fully register.

Pierre stood in the middle of the street with the thin, bearded man in a green jacket at his side. One of the man's hands was gripping Pierre's arm, the other held a knife. Neither of them seemed to be aware of the pickup truck, gathering speed as it barreled toward them.

Sam's heart somersaulted, but the blonde reacted first.

One minute she was standing beside him and the next she was sprinting toward the two men with the poodle at her side.

Sam sprang to his feet and leaped toward the curb, but she was ahead of him by two lengths. He was going to be too late. The truck was going to hit her—it was going to mow down all three of them. The dead certainty of that struck him, just as he saw something flash. Then two things happened simultaneously. The woman leapt toward the two men, using the impact of her body to shove them backward. And the truck swerved in his direction.

Fear fisting in his throat, Sam pivoted and threw himself at the hood of a parked car. Metal screeched against metal and sparks flew as the truck sideswiped the car and sent him rolling onto the sidewalk.

Scrambling to his feet, Sam placed a hand against the car for balance and managed to get the plate number before the pickup took the corner on two wheels. Then he shifted his gaze to the two figures lying in the street.

They were still, both of them, and the dog was racing around them in circles, barking.

Both…?

Glancing down the street, he spotted the thin, bearded man racing down the sidewalk.

"Stop!" His voice sounded raw and thin, and the man paid him no heed.

"Mr. Romano? What's going on?"

"I wish the hell I knew," Sam replied to Luis's voice in his ear. "There's a bearded man running down 75th Street. Luis, you take him. Tyrone, you call 911. I'm staying with Rabaut."

It wasn't until he reached his godfather and knelt down that he saw the blood. It was smeared on the woman's hand, but it seemed to be coming from a thin surface wound on

Pierre's arm. Even as he found the blonde's pulse she was pushing herself up.

He was gripping just her wrist when his eyes met hers, and his last coherent thought was that he'd never seen eyes that color. They reminded him of violets, the kind his brother grew in pots on the roof of the hotel. The punch he felt in his gut was stronger this time and set off a flood of feelings. For the life of him, he couldn't have named any of them. Because his mind, suddenly blank as a slate, had room for only one thought.

This is her.

THIS IS HIM.

The moment the thought slipped into her mind, A.J. tried to shove it out. But the words became a permanent chant in her brain, low and thrumming.

This is him. This is him.

Even then, she might have been more successful in dismissing the thought if it weren't for the feelings tumbling through her—delight, terror, recognition.

This just couldn't be him—the person that was supposed to be drawn to her by the skirt. But Claire's words flooded into her mind. "Perhaps it will get you a date with a tall, dark, handsome stranger." The description had made her think of this man—a street person. He did have dark hair and eyes, both the color of dark chocolate. And he was handsome all right. She'd noticed that the first time she'd seen him. It would have taken more than a few days' growth of beard to disguise the lean handsome features, the strong jaw. And the mouth. The lips were thin. They wouldn't be soft when they pressed against hers. They would be hard and demanding.

And it was absolutely ridiculous to be thinking of that. Her only thought when she'd slipped money into his cup and tried to find him a job was to help him. What in the world was wrong with her? Blinking hard, she tried to drag her gaze away from his.

"Are you all right?" he asked.

"Fine," she managed, shocked to find she had to work to form the words.

"That pickup nearly hit you."

The pickup. Images suddenly began to flood back into her mind—the two men had seemed so far away, the roar of the engine so close. There'd been no time to calculate the distance, to even know if she had a chance. She could still recall the impact as she'd hurled herself against the two men, and then they'd tumbled to the pavement and the breath had suddenly left her body.

That had to be why she'd suddenly felt so strange, why looking into this man's eyes had affected her in such a strange way. Relief surged through her.

"Adrenaline rush," she said.

"Pardon?"

"I felt a little strange there for a moment. Adrenaline rush. I've read that it can have a very strange effect on one's system. But I'm recovering." And she was. She even finally managed to drag her eyes away from the stranger's. And, for the first time, she saw the blood on one of the men she'd launched herself at. "You're bleeding," she said as she met the older man's eyes.

"It's just a scratch," he said, smiling up at her. "It will heal...unless I am dead and I'm staring into the eyes of an angel."

"No, you're not dead." She noted that he had a French accent and the kindest blue eyes. They were clear and focused on hers. No adrenaline surge this time. "But you took a pretty hard fall."

"I'm fine," the older man said. "It's even better if you're not an angel."

A.J. blinked. Could he be flirting with her? No. Quickly, she made herself look back at the street person. "We should help him sit up."

When he grinned at her, she began to feel another pump of adrenaline surge through her system. He had the kind of smile that made you want to smile right back.

"I'd be happy to help you with him if you'd let go of my hands," he said.

"What?"

"You've got my hands."

Glancing down, A.J. saw that her hands were indeed clasping his tightly—right there in her lap—right on top of the skirt!

"Sorry." She released him immediately, and together they eased the older man into a sitting position. Then Cleo offered her a welcome distraction by moving onto her lap and licking her face.

"We've got to be fast, Pierre." The street person's voice was low and urgent. "Give me the Abelard necklace."

A.J. managed to peer around Cleo to see that the homeless man was patting down the Frenchman.

"You are mistaken. I don't have the necklace, Salvatore."

"Salvatore?" A.J. glanced from one to the other. "Pierre? You know each other?"

"Yes," the Frenchman said, turning toward her with a smile. "Salvatore's father and I were old friends. Salvatore works for a security firm now, and he's made a little mistake."

"The name is Sam," the street person said. "Turn over the necklace, Pierre. I can't let you do this."

A.J. cut Sam off by grabbing both of his wrists. "You don't

have any right to search this man." She turned to Pierre. "Insist that he stop."

"I insist that you stop."

"I insist that you stop also," A.J. said.

Sam lifted both of his hands in the air, palms out. "Fine. But the police will be here soon." He paused so that the sirens in the distance could emphasize his point. Then he met A.J.'s eyes.

"If you want to help my godfather, you'll let me handle this."

She lifted her chin. "Really? And I'm supposed to trust the word of a thief?"

"I'm not a thief," Sam said, fishing out a card and handing it to her. "I'm a licensed private investigator and I work for Sterling Security."

"S. Romano," A.J. read aloud. "Well, Mr. Salvatore Sam Romano, no matter who you work for, you're a thief. You stole twenty dollars from me each time you let me put money in your cup."

Fishing a card out of her purse, she turned to the Frenchman. "You shouldn't say one more word to anyone until your lawyer is present. If you want, I can represent you until then."

"I would like that very much, madame—or is it mademoiselle?"

Scrambling to her feet, she helped the older man to his.

The mistake Sam made was looking at A.J. again. The thigh-high stockings had not been a figment of his imagination. The hem of her skirt had hiked up so that the lacy border of the stockings was quite visible along with a narrow expanse of smooth skin...

A.J. hurriedly pulled the skirt down, but not before Sam felt his throat go dry.

Pierre captured her left hand. "Ah. No rings. It's Mademoiselle Potter then, I presume?"

Sam stared at Pierre. He had some smooth moves for a man who had to be in his seventies.

A.J. frowned a little. "I'm not married, if that's what you mean."

"Excellent," Pierre murmured, raising her hand to his lips. "The gods have smiled on me twice today. Perhaps they will smile a third time, mademoiselle. Tell me that you are free, that there is some hope of my winning your hand."

"I hate to interrupt the romance, Pierre," Sam said. The sirens were growing closer. "But we don't have much time. When the police get here, they're going to invite you down to the station to take your statement. A man stabbed you and another one nearly ran you down. We have a very small window of opportunity here to put that necklace back. I don't want you to go to jail."

Pierre waved his free hand in a dismissive gesture. "What matter is that? The important thing is that I have just fallen in love with Mademoiselle Potter."

A.J. and Sam were still staring at Pierre when the first patrol car, sirens blaring, screeched to a halt at the curb.

2

"HAVE I TOLD YOU LATELY how much I hate smooth-talking attorneys?" Sam nudged a pile of papers aside, making a small space for himself on the corner of his brother's desk. When he unearthed a donut, he broke off a piece. He could always depend on a cop to have food nearby, and he was starved.

"Join the club. Do you want to tell me why you happened to be on the scene when Pierre was nearly run down by a truck in front of that museum?"

With a muffled curse, Sam spit the contents of his mouth into an overflowing wastebasket, then grabbed for his brother's coffee. Pure survival instinct had him glancing in the paper cup and taking a good sniff before he downed the contents. "I didn't know a donut could become mummified."

"Weird science. Happens all the time around here. Cops don't have the luxury of being neat freaks like P.I.s. And you're not answering my question."

Sam let his gaze sweep the large room that was home to the detective division. Most of the desks were cluttered, none to the extent his brother's was. But then, Andrew Jackson Romano was one of the best detectives in the city. "What do you know about the Abelard necklace?"

Andrew's brows shot up. "Just what I read in the papers. It's worth about five million, and the LaBrecque family, producers of LaBrecque Estates Bottled Wines, brought it to

New York and are exhibiting it at the Grenelle Museum to launch the new line of wines they are exporting to the U.S. Let me guess. You were part of the extra security that the papers claimed was hired to protect it."

"I think it was stolen this morning."

Andrew frowned. "No one called it in."

Stuffing his hands in his pockets, Sam paced to the window and then turned. "That's because it's in the display case. I saw it myself." Immediately after the squad car had arrived on the scene, a TV reporter with a cameraman had showed. They'd come to photograph the necklace in its case. The attempted hit-and-run had been a bonus for them.

Once Pierre and A. J. Potter had left in the squad car for the precinct, Sam had gone into the museum himself to check. And there it had been.

Andrew settled back in his chair. "It's still in the case in the museum, but you think it's been stolen. Okay, I'll bite. Why?"

"This is off the record? Brother to brother?"

Andrew's eyes narrowed. "Sure."

"I saw Pierre Rabaut climb in the skylight at six thirty-five and walk out the front door of the Grenelle at seven-forty, and I don't believe he went in for a private viewing."

"But you said it was still in the case."

"Pierre's trademark as a thief was to leave a high-quality copy in place of the jewelry he stole. That's why he was never put away. Often the theft wasn't discovered until years later, if at all. I have to talk to him. And his attorney is telling him not to talk to me."

Andrew was quiet for a minute, studying his brother. Finally he said, "Okay. Let's back up a little, and stick to the facts. What we know for sure is that Pierre was nearly run down in front of the museum."

"And he was cut on the arm by a thin man with a beard."

"Right. The mugger who got away." Andrew began to rifle through the papers on his desk. "I just ran the license plate you gave me on the pickup. Where the hell is it?"

As his brother dug into the debris, Sam turned back to the window. On the street below, cars inched their way along, and a taxi nearly lost a fender as it nosed its way to the curb.

He might have had the problem solved by now if it hadn't been for A. J. Potter. The sweet little thing who'd been giving him money and finding him a job had turned into a tough little firebrand, standing like a guardian angel over his godfather. If it hadn't been for her, he'd have had time to find the necklace and it could have been back in the museum by now. But when she'd grabbed his hands to keep him from searching Pierre, she'd absolutely drained his mind.

The woman was different for him. Oh, he'd felt desire before—even that instant and inexplicable kind he'd felt for A.J. the first time he'd seen her walking up the street toward him. But today had been different. When she'd grabbed his hands, what he'd felt then hadn't been merely desire. It had been...recognition. *This is her.* His father had warned him that he'd know when he found the woman he would fall in love with.

The moment the thought entered his mind, Sam shoved it out. No, that just wasn't a possibility. A. J. Potter was not the kind of woman he was looking for. He'd had Luis go back to the office and run a check on her. She came from the kind of money that someone earned about five generations ago, and she worked at a law firm that her great-great-grandfather had founded. His name and hers were on the letterhead of Hancock, Potter and King. In short, A.J. came from the same kind of highbrow lineage as the woman his father had fallen in love with—Isabelle Sheridan, the rich CEO of her family's company. She and his father had come from different worlds, and Sam had viewed firsthand the problems that could arise in that kind of relationship.

A sudden tingling in his fingers had Sam clenching his hands into fists. As if he'd conjured her up, A. J. Potter appeared on the street below him holding on to Pierre's arm and guiding him down the steps of the precinct. Sam frowned. The older man had some *very* interesting techniques. He knew for a fact that Pierre worked out four times a week at the same gym Sam went to. His godfather needed help getting down steps about as much as Andrew did. She laughed at something Pierre said and for a moment, as she tilted her head back, her eyes met Sam's and held.

The pull was there. Even at a distance and through glass, he could feel it. What in hell was it about her? Was it because she'd been so sweet to a person she'd thought was homeless? Or maybe his hormones had just time-warped themselves back to adolescence. Whatever the hell it was, he was going to find out. And he was going to talk to his godfather.

A.J. WAS SURPRISED at the effort it took to pull her gaze away from Mr. S. Romano. Just about as hard as it was to keep from thinking about him. Why?

Perhaps because Sam Romano wasn't what he seemed. He certainly wasn't one of New York City's homeless. In spite of that laid-back charm he'd projected when he'd conned her out of a hundred bucks, he was as stubborn as they came. And, for some reason, he was obsessed with the idea that her client was a thief.

"He's a fascinating young man," Pierre Rabaut said.

"Who?" A.J. said, forcing her complete attention to the man who was raising her hand to his lips with one hand and petting Cleo with the other.

"My godson, Salvatore." Pierre lowered her hand but kept it in his. "His father Henry and I were very close until he passed away two years ago. We came to this country about the same time. Henry worked for me at my jazz club until he got enough money to open his hotel, Henry's Place. I've known all the Romano boys—Nick, Tony, Andrew and Sam—since they were babes. Sam was always the cleverest of the lot. The youngest sometimes has to be, no?"

"I suppose. Why does your godchild want to put you in jail?"

When Cleo flopped to the sidewalk and rolled over, Pierre leaned down to scratch her on her neck. The poodle's tongue dangled out of the side of her mouth as she slipped into dog heaven. "He doesn't. But he's a man of principle. He's been hired to see that the necklace isn't stolen, and he believes I've done just that. I think he wants to convince me to put it back."

A.J. studied her client. Although his hair was both thinning and gray, she would have guessed him to be in his early sixties if he hadn't told her he was seventy-five. A thin, wiry man, he moved with a grace and agility that reminded her of Fred Astaire dancing with Ginger Rogers in late-night movies she'd seen. And there was a keen intelligence in his dark blue eyes.

"But you didn't steal it. The necklace is still in the museum."

"Yes," Pierre agreed. "It is."

Cleo chose that moment to roll over. Immediately, Pierre obligingly scratched her belly. "She's a lovely dog."

"You're being very patient with her. Cleo throws herself at every male she meets—man or beast, except for the pedigreed studs her mistress matches her up with. My roommates and I think she has all the makings of a slut."

Pierre chuckled as he continued to stroke Cleo. "She has a great desire to be loved, that's all. Some women deal with it by throwing themselves at men. Others deal with it by isolating themselves and pushing men away. All this beauty needs is to be loved by the right male. I ought to introduce her to my dog, Antoine."

"No, please don't. Not unless he's a pure-bred poodle and registered at some kennel club. Otherwise, Mrs. Higgenbotham, her owner, will have my head."

"Ahhh." Rising to his feet, Pierre shook his head sadly. "So there's an arranged marriage in Mademoiselle Cleo's future. Too bad. They often result in tragedy. It is much wiser to follow your heart—if you have the courage."

A.J. studied him for a moment as he continued to stroke the dog. She could have sworn that he was talking about more than Cleo's problems.

A limousine pulled up to the curb and, as the driver alighted, Pierre continued to pet the dog absently. "Salvatore is going to insist on talking to me. He's always had a fascination for solving puzzles. He keeps after them, like a dog with a bone."

A.J.'s eyes narrowed as she thought for a minute. "Why don't I arrange a meeting then? That way I can make sure I'll be present."

"Yes. That would be best." Smiling, Pierre raised her hand to his lips again. "I have always had a weakness for beauty and brains in a woman, Mademoiselle Potter. And you remind me of someone I knew a long time ago."

For a moment, A.J. said nothing. She could see that her client had drifted away into a memory, and she saw traces of both joy and grief in his eyes. Then, suddenly, they cleared and she could read nothing in them.

"How about later this afternoon—say, around five o'clock?" Pierre suggested. "There's a small café called Emile's. It's near the courthouse and they serve excellent

French coffee. Their wine list is superb. I think you would enjoy it."

"That would be fine," A.J. said.

Pierre raised her hand to his lips again. "And you'll let Salvatore know?"

"Absolutely."

A.J. waited until the driver of the limo had settled Pierre into his seat and closed the door before turning on her heel and marching up the precinct steps. A meeting with her client wasn't the only thing A.J. intended to settle with Mr. Salvatore Sam Romano.

"EARTH TO SAM. Come in, Sam."

"Sorry." Sam turned back from the window to face his brother. "What were you saying?"

"I found the license plate number. It belongs to a pickup owned by a construction company. They reported it stolen this morning."

"So it wasn't an accident," Sam said as he took the scrap of paper and tucked it in a pocket.

"Probably not," Andrew said as he studied his brother. "Hit-and-run drivers don't like to use their own vehicles. You got any other evidence that Pierre might have copped the necklace—other than that he often left copies when he pulled a heist?"

"That and the fact that I saw him break and enter the museum. He's good enough to have jammed the security cameras and he obviously turned off the alarms."

"Damn," Andrew said.

"I think it's safe to say that he didn't do all that to have a private viewing of the exhibits. He may have the real necklace on him right now."

Leaning back, Andrew propped his feet on the desk. "Why? For the past forty years, Pierre Rabaut has lived in this city and been a model citizen. He operates a highly successful and lucrative jazz club and serves on a couple of the mayor's committees. Why go back to a life of crime now?"

"Yeah," Sam said. "I was thinking about that while he was in the museum. He was really good at stealing, you know. One of the best. Maybe he just wanted to see if he could still do it."

"It's a hell of a solution to a mid-life crisis. And what about the man with the knife and the guy in the pickup? How do they fit in?"

"Pierre knew there was extra security. It was on the news. I figure the bearded mugger was an accomplice. He was supposed to take the necklace and run. That way Pierre couldn't be caught with the necklace on him. The guy in the pickup is another matter. He was out to get Pierre. And he must have known Pierre would be there. All I know for sure is that as long as Pierre has the necklace, he's in danger."

Andrew thought for a minute. "We only have your word. That's not probable cause to search him."

"That's the last thing I want. What I want is to convince him to return the necklace before he gets caught, and Ms. A. J. Potter won't let me near him."

Andrew's eyes widened. "Ms. A. J. Potter? Pierre has a woman attorney, and you're having trouble getting around her?"

"She's—" Rising, Sam began to pace again. "You should have seen her when she saw that truck barreling toward Pierre and the bearded man. She's this tiny little bit of a thing, and she didn't even stop to think. She moved like lightning and launched herself at them." Even now when he thought about it, fear knotted in his stomach. "I thought they were all goners. I couldn't believe it when the truck swerved at the last minute. It was a miracle."

"A. J. Potter, hmm?" Andrew's face split into a wide grin. "Nice name. Same initials as me. I suppose she's a looker too?"

"Yeah. She's..." Sam paused. It occurred to him that he'd never before had trouble talking about a woman to his brother. But he didn't feel comfortable talking about A.J.'s legs—or any other part of her. And he certainly wasn't going to tell his brother that her eyes reminded him of violets. "She's...I...she's hard to describe."

"I can see that. She's got you stuttering."

"No...I mean..."

"Is she single?"

Sam frowned. "Yeah. Pierre got that out of her in less than two minutes. For a guy in his seventies, he's got a way with women. He told her he'd fallen in love with her. What kind of a thing is that to tell a girl first time you meet her?"

"You better introduce us, bro. Maybe she and I will have more in common than the initials."

Sam pinned his brother with a long, steady look. "Forget it."

"This just keeps getting better and better. First you're jealous of an old man. Now you're warning me off. I've got to meet her."

"No." Just as Sam's fingers began to tingle, Andrew gave a long, low whistle.

"Too late. We've got company."

Sam knew before he turned who it was moving toward him. He would have recognized the click of those heels and that quick, ground-eating stride anywhere. The moment he turned, he got a quick vision of a woman and poodle before his eyes homed in and fastened like a tractor beam to her legs. The skirt seemed to inch a little higher with each step she took. He felt the blood drain from his head.

A.J. VERY NEARLY STOPPED mid-stride. If Cleo hadn't been pulling at her leash she might have. This time the rush of adrenaline surged through her and he wasn't even touching her. It was his eyes. He looked at her in a way that no one else did—as if he could really see her.

"Two things," A.J. said when she reached him. In a minute, she would remember what they were. She drew in a deep breath and opened her mouth, hoping that something intelligent would come out.

He spoke first. "I want to see my godfather."

"Right. That's number one on my list. He wants to meet with you at a French café, Emile's, near the courthouse at five this afternoon."

The smile came then, quick and charming. She wanted to smile right back, but she bit down on the side of her cheek instead. Ruthlessly, she gathered the evidence against him. This was a man who wanted to put a defenseless old man in jail. A man who had with that same charming smile taken money from her on the street!

"Number two," lifting her hand, she turned it palm up, "I also want my money back."

"Your money...?"

"The hundred dollars I've slipped into your cup during the past five days."

"Whoa," Sam said, holding his hands up in a gesture of surrender. "I gave all of it to a homeless man who hangs around my family's hotel. He might be interested in that job you were lining up for me."

She studied him for a moment. "If you're making fun—"

In a movement that she didn't even see coming, he took the hand she was still extending and began to draw her toward the door. "Me, make fun? Never. Why don't I buy you a cup of coffee and we can talk about the money and Pierre?"

"I've got some coffee right here," Andrew said, snagging

her other hand and putting a mug of coffee in it. "And I have some information on that pickup that tried to run down your client."

IT WAS ONE OF THOSE TIMES when Sam wished he'd been an only child. Or that murdering your brother was legal. One minute, he'd nearly had A.J. out the door for a private chat and, the next, Andrew had drawn her back to his desk. He'd even cleaned off a chair for her.

"This is a really nice dog you've got there," Andrew said. "Do you show him...or is it a her?"

Andrew was actually petting the dog. Even more amazing was that his desk was also looking more orderly. File folders were stacked in a pile, and Sam could even make out the edge of a pristine-looking blotter. He was sure it had never seen the light of day before. But what really stunned him was that he hadn't been aware that any of that was going on. All he'd been aware of was A. J. Potter from the moment she'd walked into the room.

"Cleo is a her. And she loves men. My neighbor shows her. Right now she's looking for the perfect male to breed her with."

"My brother has absolutely no manners." Andrew managed to get Cleo settled on his lap. "Otherwise, he'd introduce us. I'm Andrew Jackson Romano, but you can call me Andrew." He took A.J.'s hand in his. "We have the same initials."

Murder was out of the question. But he'd warned Andrew off. In a minute, he was going to punch him. He hadn't felt that way since junior high school. Hell, it couldn't be jealousy he was feeling. Could it? But as two other detectives rose from their desks and gravitated toward A.J., Sam had the sinking realization that it was. And that was ridiculous.

A. J. Potter shook her head. "No coffee, thanks. I'm very

late for a meeting at my office. My client asked me to give Mr. Romano a message. And I just wanted to clear up the money thing." She glanced at Sam, then back at his brother. "Is he telling the truth? Did he give my hundred dollars to a homeless person?"

"I'll be happy to check into it for you."

"Andrew..." The warning note in Sam's voice was clear.

Andrew sighed. "You can always take Sam at his word, Ms. Potter."

A.J. nodded. Then she plucked the poodle off Andrew's lap, turned to Sam and gave him the same brief nod. "Two more things. First, I won't press charges for the money. And two, I don't want you harassing my client anymore. He said you'd have questions. We'll settle them this afternoon, and then you'll leave him alone. Understood?"

The two brothers watched her until the door swung shut and blocked her from their view.

"Very nice. If that skirt had inched up just a little bit—"

Sam whirled on his brother.

"Hey! I'm just admiring the view. She's—"

"Yes...?"

Andrew cleared his throat. "In the interest of brotherly love and support, it's only fair to tell you that if you decide you don't want her, I'm calling second dibs."

Sam frowned. "I don't want..." He stopped short, stunned, when he found he couldn't complete the sentence.

Andrew grinned at him. "See? You'd have known it sooner if you were as good a detective as I am."

Sam didn't comment. He had too much to think about as he headed toward the door.

GLANCING AT HER WATCH, A.J. raced down the steps of the precinct building with Cleo in tow. Ten o'clock. She'd lost another five minutes delivering her client's message to Sam

Romano. But Pierre had insisted. And he *was* her client. Her very first. She might have danced a little jig on the sidewalk if it weren't for the fact that landing her first client had caused her to miss the monthly meeting at the firm.

Unless... Fishing out her cell phone, she punched in her uncle's number, then kept her voice as patient as she could as she waited for the receptionist to route the call. A quick scan of the street told her there were no taxis in waving range, so she drew Cleo with her toward the corner.

There was a chance, a slim one, that she hadn't missed the meeting entirely. But that hope was dashed when her uncle's secretary Mrs. Scranton immediately put the call through.

"Ari—oh, sorry, I forgot. No one is allowed to call you that anymore."

A.J. drew in a deep breath the moment she recognized her cousin's voice. Rodney was the only one in the family who needled her about the fact that she'd changed her name legally to A.J. She'd done it before she went to college. To her, the name Arianna conjured up images of all the pink dresses and formal afternoon tea parties she'd endured to please her Aunt Margery. In college and law school she'd wanted to project an entirely different image. A.J. was a much better name for the tough lawyer she'd intended to become.

"Rodney, don't tell me. Let me guess. Uncle Jamison announced his retirement and the board appointed you the new head of the firm. That's why you've moved into your dad's office."

"I'll be running this place sooner than you think. I'm going to be working with Father on the Parker Ellis Chase file. In a few months, it will be mine."

"Congratulations." A.J. tamped down the feelings running through her. Jealousy was a waste of time, and disappointment...well, she could eventually do something to change that. Parker Ellis Chase ran a fifty-million-a-year company that was constantly running into problems with the EPA. The file was an up-and-coming litigator's dream.

"You were on TV. We caught it at the end of the news. Dad wants to see you as soon as you get here. A hit-and-run?" He made a clicking sound with his tongue. "It's bad enough that you're dragging in those ragtag pro bono clients from the overflow at the Public Defender's office, but a hit-and-run? Father is not pleased."

"Thanks for the update, Rodney. Did anything get thrown my way at the meeting?"

"You got quite a few research requests. I put the files on your desk myself."

Careful to keep the disappointment out of her voice, A.J. said, "Thanks. I'll be in shortly."

The one disadvantage cell phones had over the wired kind was that you couldn't slam them in someone's ear. As she tucked the phone in her pocket and once more searched the street for a taxi, Cleo made a low sound in her throat.

"I know, sweetie. You're very late for your appointment, but I called Dr. Fielding, and he's going to squeeze you in."

Out of habit, she glanced around. A few pedestrians milled past them, hurrying to cross the street before the light changed. But there was no sign of another dog. She did catch a glimpse of Sam Romano coming out of the front door of the precinct, and she quickly strode away from him toward the corner.

Just as they reached it, Cleo growled deep in her throat and then barked.

The shove from behind took A.J. by surprise and sent her sprawling to her knees. Then the man grabbed her arm and jerked her to her feet. With her free hand, she grabbed the strap of her purse, swung it off her shoulder and into the man's face. The moment he dropped her arm, she aimed and landed a quick kick to his stomach.

With a string of curses, he sank to his knees, but he caught the strap of her purse and held on. In the second that their eyes met and held, A.J. sized him up. He was thin, with a beard, but there were muscles under that frayed gray T-shirt and a grim determination in his eyes.

"You're not getting my purse," she said, pulling on the strap.

Suddenly, he was on his feet, moving backward and yanking her forward with sharp tugs on her purse. She stumbled, and for a minute, she was sure she'd lose her balance.

Cleo raced in from behind and nipped at his ankles.

"Damn!" He kicked at the dog and nearly lost his balance.

Pressing her advantage, A.J. dug in her heels and jerked backward. The man went down to one knee. He used his free hand to swing at Cleo and then clamped it on her wrist. Out of the corner of her eye, A.J. saw the dog skitter back out of reach.

"C'mon, lady. You're...you're..."

He stopped talking entirely then. He even stopped moving, and A.J. saw that he was staring at her skirt. Do your work, she thought, swaying her hips a little as she recalled the way Samantha had worked the skirt's magic on Tavish. *Please, do your work.* But when she tugged on her purse, he didn't loosen his grip.

Damn! She didn't want the guy magnetized to her. She wanted him unmagnetized.

"Let...go!" A.J. pulled tight on the strap and prayed it wouldn't rip.

The man still didn't budge. It was almost as if he'd been turned into a statue.

She felt her arms begin to tremble. Clearly, she wasn't going to win the tug-of-war, so she opted for intimidation instead. "Look, buddy. Let go while you still can. I'll be able to ID you in a line-up. You'll go to jail."

He moved then, lifting his head and meeting her eyes. With all her strength she jerked on the strap, then suddenly pitched backward and, with the purse clutched to her chest, landed smack on her backside. She had a moment to register the pain shooting through her. Then she saw the thin, bearded man racing down the street with Cleo and Sam Romano in hot pursuit.

"Cleo, stop!" She couldn't allow anything to happen to the dog. Scrambling to her feet, she raced after them.

"STOP!"

As Sam careened around the corner, he risked a quick look back to confirm that A. J. Potter was up and running after them. Admiration warred with fury. Either was a welcome replacement for the fear that had shot through him when he'd realized that A.J. was being attacked by the same man who had knifed Pierre Rabaut in front of the museum.

He shifted his gaze back to his quarry, dodging to the left to miss a lady loaded with shopping bags. The thin guy knew how to race through a crowded street, zigging and zagging to hit as few pedestrians as possible. It was a skill cops, P.I.s and muggers had to be good at. And dogs, he thought as he caught sight of the poodle shooting between someone's legs to his right.

Ahead, the guy dodged to the left of the stream of people hurrying across the intersection and turned the corner. Swearing under the short, shallow breaths he was dragging in, Sam sprinted to close the distance. The moment he skidded around the corner, his worst fears were confirmed. He was looking down one of the narrow side streets that crossed Manhattan, and right now it was choked with traffic. A delivery truck, parked on the sidewalk in front of him was blocking his view. Tearing around it, Sam spotted the thin man about fifty paces ahead. He ran in a straight path through the bottlenecked vehicles, focusing all his attention on catching his man.

Sounds exploded around him—the blare of horns, the shouts of curses. He kept his gaze on his quarry.

"Cleo!"

It had to be his imagination. That couldn't be A. J. Potter's voice. She couldn't possibly have kept up with him. Out of the corner of his eye, he caught a glimpse of the poodle on the sidewalk. And ahead of the dog, the bearded man was lengthening the distance between them again.

Sweat poured down his forehead, and as he swept it out of his eyes, he saw the man duck into an alley. Sam tore between a pickup and a limousine, then barely missed colliding with a biker. The alley was dark and in the moment it took for his eyes to adjust, he heard a splintering crate and saw the rolling river of head lettuce just in time to leap over it. Lungs bursting, he raced forward. He could see the man ahead of him, a dark silhouette against the bright light at the end of the alley, and he was gaining.

DRAGGING IN AIR, A.J. dodged an oncoming pedestrian and hugged the edge of the sidewalk as she tore down the street. Ahead of her she saw Cleo disappear into an alley and fear sprinted through her. If something happened to her…

No. Ruthlessly, she pushed the thought away and put all her energy into the run. At the mouth of the alley, she took a sharp left and found herself ankle deep in rolling head lettuce. Kicking them out of her way, she plunged forward and tried to locate the dog in the sudden gloom.

"Cleo!" Her voice was thready, her heart nearly beating its way out of her chest as she picked up the pace. Lungs burning, she squinted, willing her eyes to adjust until she finally spotted two darker shapes near the end of the alley. Cleo had to be there. She had to be.

SAM SWORE. The light ahead darkened as a truck began to back slowly across the opening at the end of the alley. He put all he could into his sprint, but he was still twenty yards behind when he saw his quarry slip through the small crack of light that was left. He shot out his hands to break his crash into the side of the truck.

Then dropping to his knees, he dragged in air as he weighed his chances of crawling under the truck and continuing the chase. The sight of the railing leading down to the subway told him it would be a waste of time. Any guy as savvy as the thin bearded man seemed to be would have lost himself in the crowds below ground by now.

Pushing himself to his feet, he leaned one arm against the truck and prayed that he could get enough air into his lungs.

"Cleo!"

He whirled in time to catch A.J. as she flew into him.

FOR A MOMENT, all A.J. could do was concentrate on taking deep, cleansing breaths. But the moment enough oxygen got to her brain, she looked frantically around for the dog. "Cleo!"

"She's right here."

And there she was, sitting right next to them, her tongue hanging out, every bit as desperate for air as they were.

As relief surged through her, A.J. became aware that Sam had his arms around her. His heart was beating against her ear. She felt that same kind of heightened awareness that she had in front of the museum, but not that same kind of zinging excitement she'd felt before. This time she felt...at home in Sam Romano's arms.

This is him.

No. It was the adrenaline again. A man had just tried to steal her purse. She'd very nearly lost Cleo on the streets of New York.

"The man—" A.J. pushed herself back from Sam's chest.

"He got away. You know, you can really run."

It was a mistake to look up at him. He was big, taller than she'd been aware of before. And she couldn't seem to drag her eyes away as his lips curved into a smile. It was the same one he'd given her before—the one that tempted her to smile right back at him. "Thanks."

"I bet you ran track in school."

Surprised, she met his eyes. "Cross country. I'm lousy at sprints."

"But you can hang in there for the distance. That's what counts. And you work out too. Weights, I'll bet."

She nodded. It struck her as an odd conversation to be having in an alley with a man who was holding her in his arms, a man whose mouth was only inches away from hers. A man whose eyes were so deep, so dark...

She couldn't stay here. The fact that she wanted to, that whatever else it was she had to do wasn't nearly as important, should have frightened her.

"Mr. Romano..." she began, but she couldn't seem to find any other words. There were too many sensations streaming through her—the press of his fingers at her back, the hardness of his chest, the strength of his arms. And the sudden heat that they seemed to be making together.

"I want to kiss you."

For a second A.J. wasn't sure who said the words. The thought had been in her mind. Her body had already started to respond to it, softening, fitting itself to the hard angles and planes of his. But a sane little voice in her head was objecting.

"You...we shouldn't."

She watched his lips curve again.

"A *no* might have stopped me. But not a *shouldn't.* I always like to do the things I shouldn't do, don't you?"

His breath was so warm on her lips, so tempting.

"Stand up on your tiptoes," he whispered.

She did exactly what he asked, and he brushed his lips across hers, then withdrew.

She moved her hands to the back of his neck and drew him closer until their lips were brushing again.

"More?" he asked.

3

OH, SHE DEFINITELY WANTED MORE.

The kiss had begun so softly, his lips just nibbling hers and tasting. It shouldn't have been enough to make her blood grow thick, her muscles go lax or her knees turn to water. Still, A.J. could have testified she felt each one of those things happen in quick succession—just as if someone were throwing a series of light switches. Then he nipped her bottom lip and whatever reservations she still harbored about not kissing Sam Romano clicked off, too.

This is him.

Again the words slipped into her mind and became a chant. In a minute, she would ignore them. Right now she couldn't think of anything but tasting him—sampling more of the dark, male flavor of him. Moving even higher on her toes, she wrapped her arms around his neck and pulled him closer.

Then, at last, his lips grew harder and hotter on hers. When his tongue finally tangled with hers, the flavors turned sharper, and she tasted hunger, a hint of desperation—his or her own, she didn't know which.

This was the way she'd always dreamed of being kissed—sometime by someone. It was familiar and new at the same time. Never before had she had this sudden need to get closer. Nor had she ever experienced the delight that was bubbling through her.

The intensity was new too. She was so aware of the

strength of his hands and the press of each of his fingers against the side of her face and her back. He touched her nowhere else and yet it was as if he touched every part of her. Only his mouth moved on hers, yet desire moved through her until it hurt.

OH, YES. *This is her.*

Each time the thought slipped into his mind, Sam was finding it harder and harder to uproot it. Her lips were so incredibly soft, so moist. He withdrew just enough to nip her bottom lip with his teeth, then to absorb the sweet ache of power when he heard the quick catch of her breath.

Oh, yes. Definitely more.

He'd wanted to kiss her—it seemed like forever. From that first time she'd stopped and put money in his cup? But she'd been right about one thing. He shouldn't have done it. Not here. Not now. Because he'd started something that he couldn't finish. He had to stop, but he couldn't. In a minute, maybe. Her mouth was so pliant, so warm, so incredibly generous. And her taste—it was everything he'd ever dreamed of—sweetness laced with a deep, ripe passion. He couldn't get enough of it. And she seemed to know just how to meet his demands before he thought to make them.

They might be in an alley, but when he drew in a ragged breath, he caught the scent of a summer breeze. Though it was concrete he stood on, he could have sworn that he felt the ground shifting under his feet like sand.

He scraped his teeth over her bottom lip, and her moan rippled through his system. Though it cost him, he kept one hand at the side of her face, the other pressed against her back. He wanted too much to touch her—to slip her out of that yellow blazer, to push her shirt off her shoulders and then let his hands mold slowly, very, very slowly, every inch of her. Then he would slip his hand beneath that skirt...Sam could feel his mind emptying as surely and as quickly as if someone had just pulled out a stopper.

He was in trouble. He didn't need the tingling in his fingers to tell him that.

Big trouble. It wasn't as though he'd never gotten himself in a jam before. He had. But he'd always made sure he had an escape route.

But a man had to want to use it. A man had to have the strength to step back from the edge of a cliff. All he wanted was to keep on kissing her.

"Hey!"

The shout freed him from the paralysis that seemed to grip him. At the same moment he registered the sharp barking of a dog.

"Hey!"

He glanced over his shoulder at the burly man who was moving toward them.

"A.J.," he said as he carefully moved his hands to her arms and shifted her away from the truck. He hadn't even been aware that he'd pressed her against it. Stepping back, he supported her by the arms until her eyes fluttered open. They were wide, dazed and he could see himself in them. He wanted more than anything to kiss her again—and this time to take the kiss where it was meant to go.

"Is this your dog?"

Keeping an arm around A.J., Sam turned to the man. He had a short roly-poly build and a Yankee baseball cap was doing its best to hold his wiry white hair in place. "Yes, she is."

The man handed him the leash. "You should keep a better eye on her. She's been flirting with my dog, Buster. If he weren't going on sixteen, they might have already done the deed. The moment I saw three names on her collar, I figured she has to be careful who she hangs out with, if you know what I mean." The man looked from one to the other of them. "Some matches aren't meant to be. Princesses and paupers—they just don't mix."

"I catch your drift," Sam said with a nod. The guy could have been talking about A.J. and him. If anyone fit the description of princess and pauper, A.J. and he did. And from what he'd observed, the combination usually only worked out in fairy tales. It certainly hadn't worked out so well for his father. But he wasn't his father. He kept his arm around A.J.'s shoulders. "Appreciate your concern."

"No problem," the man said, winking and tipping his hat as he turned away. "I like animals. People too. Don't like to see them make unhappiness for themselves."

"An alley philosopher," Sam said. "Only in Manhattan."

"Poor Cleo," A.J. said as she patted the dog. "She's so lonely. Mrs. Higgenbotham is searching for her breeding soul mate through a kennel club, and in the meantime, she's..."

"She's frustrated," Sam supplied as they began to make their way down the alley.

"And in therapy."

Sam grinned. "You're putting me on."

"No. She's being treated for what is known as CID—Canine Intimacy Dysfunction."

"Boy, I bet you get to charge a lot to treat that."

"You got that right."

"And in laymen's terms CID means...?"

"She won't mate with the right sort at the kennel club, but she's always attracted to the wrong types. She has a case of very bad taste."

"I don't know about that." As they reached the mouth of the alley, Sam took her arm and forced her to stop. "I thought she showed good taste when she bit that bearded man in the ankle."

A.J. smiled at him then. "True. She was amazing. I didn't think she had it in her."

For a moment, as their eyes met and held, Sam simply smiled back at her. He was hot and sweaty, he'd just chased a man who'd gotten away, he was no closer to figuring out how to help his godfather, and he'd just realized he wanted a woman who was all wrong for him. He should have been feeling as frustrated as Cleo.

Instead, he felt oddly...content. And he wanted the moment to continue.

"I didn't think you had it in you either." Because he couldn't help himself, he reached out to tuck a strand of hair behind her ear. "The way you held on to your purse. Most women would have just stood there and screamed for help. A.J., I ..." Those violet eyes were weaving their spell again. He could feel words slipping away, but this time he wasn't going to let it happen. "I want to see you again. Soon. Tonight."

"No."

He shoved aside the quick stab of disappointment. "Tomorrow night then. I have this place in mind."

"No. I can't go out with you, period."

"Why not?"

"Two reasons. First of all, I represent Pierre. I don't think it would be proper for me—"

He shot her a grin as he guided her toward the mouth of the alley. "No problem. We won't talk about him. When can I pick you up? Better still," he said, scanning the street, "let's have some coffee and you can tell me where you'd like to go." The moment he spotted the small café on the corner, he took her arm and drew her toward it.

"No. Cleo's late for her therapy appointment, and I am very late for work. Plus, there's nothing to discuss. My number two reason for not going out with you is I don't date. I've had too many disasters in that arena lately."

"Then we won't talk about that either. Instead, you can tell me what the A in A.J. stands for. It's driving me nuts. You don't look like an Anne or an Allie. I'm guessing something more unusual like Athena or Aurora? Am I right?"

"No, and I—"

"Something strong like Anastasia? Antonia? Alexandra?"

"No."

"You might as well tell me. I'll just keep guessing until I get it."

"Don't be ridiculous. I have to get to work." She dug in her heels and stopped the same instant that Sam spotted the thin bearded man coming around the corner. He was talking on a cell phone. The instant the man spotted him, he pivoted back to the corner and shot off down the side street.

"C'mon." Tightening his grip on A.J., Sam raced toward the corner.

"Did you hear me? I'm not going to have coffee with you. And I'm not going on a date with you," she said. But she was keeping pace with him. The dog too.

"We're not going for coffee," Sam said as he tried to weave them through a group of people alighting from a bus. "I just saw the man who tried to snatch your purse."

"Where?"

That was a damn good question, Sam thought as they rounded the corner and he scanned the street. "There." He pointed with his free hand. "See. He's halfway down the block on the other side."

But even as they sprinted forward, the man hopped into the open door of a green van, and it shot away from the curb.

"Damn!" Sam said as he slowed to a walk. "I didn't get a good enough look at the plate. Did you?"

"No," A.J. said. "I didn't think. Do you think he was going to take another shot at my purse?"

"My question exactly. We were bound to come out this end of the alley. It's hard to believe it's just a coincidence that he was headed back toward it."

Stopping at a hot dog stand, he ordered two coffees and two hot dogs, one loaded. "I need some brain food. Are you hungry?"

A.J. STARED AT HIM. Clearly, the man had no idea how to take no for an answer. "No, I'm not hungry. And I told you before, I don't have time for coffee."

He smiled at her. "Just hold one of them for me. I'll probably need two. I was on that stakeout all night." He took the naked hot dog out of the bun and fed it to Cleo, then offered the loaded one to A.J. "Want a bite?"

The scent of mustard, onions and chili had her stomach growling. A second later she accepted the bite he was offering and let the flavors explode on her tongue. She savored them the whole time it took him to polish off the rest of the hot dog. "How can anything that is so bad for you taste so good?"

His laugh was quick and infectious. "That mixture of bad and good—it's the key ingredient in temptation. Irresistible."

A.J. studied him then. In the sunlight, with his eyes laughing at her, he was pretty tempting himself. And she had to put him, and what had happened between them in that alley, out of her mind.

Before she could say a thing, he reached out and rubbed his thumb across her bottom lip. "Mustard."

She felt the heat slide right down to her toes.

"So where do you want to go tonight?"

She gathered her scattered thoughts and said, "You are obsessed."

The grin flashed again. "I'm beginning to think so."

"Look. You may have gotten the wrong impression. That is...I may have given you the wrong impression in the alley. That kiss..."

"Pretty sensational, wasn't it? I'm looking forward to our next one."

She drew in a breath and tried again. "It...we...we can't let it happen again. We are all wrong for each other. You must be able to see that."

He was studying her, his head tilted to one side, a gleam of amusement in his eyes. "Maybe we shouldn't. But I'm predicting we'll kiss again and often. Now that we both know what it's like, it will be a powerful temptation."

The thought of what it could be like was still spinning around in her brain when, in a quick change of mood, Sam tossed his empty cup into a trash container, threw a friendly arm around her shoulder and said, "But I can wait. And now that I've had some brain food, I want to figure out why that bearded man is so intent on stealing your purse that he'd make a second try. I don't suppose Pierre slipped you the necklace and you've been carrying it around all day?"

Slipping from under his arm, A.J. signaled a taxi. "You are definitely obsessed. Pierre did not steal that necklace. When I drop Cleo off at her therapist's, I'll see if they can squeeze you in."

"Ouch. Do you treat all your dates this way?"

She waited for the taxi to cut across two lanes and pull to the curb. Then she turned to him. "Read my lips. We are not on a date now, nor will we ever be on a date."

He reached for the door of the taxi and pulled it open. The moment she and Cleo were settled, he slipped in beside her.

"What are you—?"

"Free escort service," Sam said as he slipped the taxi driver a twenty. "That's for the U-turn you're going to make."

The speed with which the cab shot from the curb and across three lanes had A.J. plastered against him. His hands were gripping her shoulders. Hers were pressed against his chest. She could feel his heart beating as quickly as hers. "You are crazy."

"Seems that way," he said as he stared into her eyes. "Obsessed and crazy. That about sums it up. Plus, I want to make it very hard for that green van to follow us."

A.J. waited, hardly daring to breathe as Sam stared at her for a long moment. She was suddenly aware of how close they were. For one humming minute she was sure he was going to kiss her again. Or she could kiss him. If either of them moved even the barest fraction of an inch, their lips would come into contact and she could experience that same whip of delight and desire that she'd experienced in the alley. Her hands were burning to reach up, to pull him closer, to—

"Where to?" the driver asked.

A.J gathered in her thoughts and gave Dr. Fielding's address on Park Avenue.

Sam eased her away from him and turned to glance out the back window.

She clenched her hands into fists. What was she thinking of? *Kissing Sam Romano in a taxi? Ripping his clothes off in a taxi? Making love to him in a taxi? All of the above.*

Good grief, she was getting as bad as Cleo. Except Cleo threw herself at *every* male. A.J. knew she'd never felt this way about any other man. Sam Romano was...different.

Lowering her hands to her lap, she flexed her fingers, then folded them together. She had to get a grip. He certainly had. He had dropped his hands from her and was totally focused on the traffic behind him. And he didn't say another word until they had dropped Cleo off for her therapy session and the taxi was headed toward the Potter Building.

When Sam turned to her, his expression was serious. "A.J., there's something I need to tell you."

"What is it?" she asked. "Did the van follow us?"

"No. But I'm betting it would be if we hadn't lost it." He raised his hand to prevent her from speaking, then continued. "Look, I believe you have my godfather's welfare at heart. So I'm going to tell you some things about Pierre Rabaut that no one else knows. I'm doing this because I think you might be in danger. I have to know that it won't go any further."

"Okay."

Sam took her hand and held it in his. "Before he retired forty years ago, Pierre was one of the best jewel thieves in Europe. That and the fact that I saw him go in through the skylight of the museum and walk out the front door lead me to believe that he stole the necklace. I want him to put it back before he gets caught."

"But—"

Sam raised a hand. "No, hear me out. I figure this bearded guy pulled a knife on Pierre in front of the museum. I told my brother I thought it was a setup. Pierre knows there's extra security, so he arranges for an accomplice to mug him as he walks out of the museum. But then the guy in the pickup interrupts the mugging. I'm betting Pierre still has the necklace. But what if the mugger isn't Pierre's accomplice and he thinks Pierre passed it to you? Or that you know where it is? In that case, the bearded man may be after you. That green van was mighty handy."

"You know, you might really be scaring me, but I feel compelled to point out to you that the necklace is still in the museum."

"There's something I didn't mention."

A.J. studied him closely. "What?"

"Pierre used to leave high-quality fakes behind so that the theft wouldn't be discovered right away."

A.J. swallowed. "No. He didn't do it. He told me that the Abelard necklace is in the museum, and I believe him."

"The bearded man evidently doesn't have the same faith in Pierre that you do. Unless there's some other reason that he might be coming after you?"

"No." A.J. felt a sudden warmth spreading through her from where their hands were still clasped. Glancing down, she saw that her knuckles had whitened because she was holding on to him so tightly. But the heat didn't seem to be coming entirely from their hands. She could have sworn some of it was coming from the skirt. Slowly, her eyes widened. "No. It couldn't be."

"What?" Sam asked.

"The skirt. Outside the precinct when we were having that tug-of-war with the purse, he did stare at it kind of strangely. For a moment, I thought it might have actually worked a kind of spell on him. But that's ridiculous."

"What is?" Sam asked.

"This skirt couldn't really have attracted a mugger."

Sam stared down at it. "Where did you get that?"

"My roommate Samantha Baldwin got it from her cousin Kate Talavera in Seattle. Supposedly, it was woven in the moonlight out of a special fiber that only grows on this island. And it—"

"Draws your true love to you."

A.J. stared at him. He wasn't telling her she was crazy. Instead, he was talking as if he ran into skirts with special man-magnet fibers every day. "Are you attempting to humor me?"

"Not at all." Glancing up, he grinned at her. "I've had dealings with this skirt before."

"You have?"

"A case I worked on last winter. The thing got written up in *Metropolitan* magazine, even made it onto a couple of talk shows. But I never got to touch it. Do you mind?"

The warmth that the skirt was generating was nothing compared to what she felt when Sam's fingers brushed against the skin on her thigh. Heat spread upward in fiery ribbons until it formed a tight fist in her stomach.

"You don't believe in it, do you?"

"What?" he asked as he continued to rub the fabric between his thumb and forefinger.

"That a fiber or something like that could draw you to your true love."

"You mean something like fate?" he asked, meeting her eyes. "My father believed in that stuff. After my mother died, he fell in love with a very rich woman—Isabelle Sheridan of the Boston Sheridans. He thought it was fate—that he'd found the one woman that he was meant to be with. It didn't work out very happily for him."

"Why not?"

Sam shrugged. "They came from different worlds. Neither one of them felt they could fit into the other one's life. So they didn't try. It kind of puts you off the whole true love thing." He smiled at her then. "But I'm very big on dating. How come you're not?"

"I thought we covered this topic."

"No. We covered why you won't date me. I'm asking why you've given it up in general. Give me your top two reasons."

"Okay. Number one, I've decided to focus on my job right now. And two, I haven't been enjoying my dates lately."

"I'll bet that's because you've been spending time with the kennel club types."

"What?"

"You know, the kind that Cleo is seeing a therapist for—multiple names, perfect breeding, impeccable manners and deadly dull?"

She had to struggle to prevent a laugh.

"You might try someone from the other side of the tracks."

A.J. met his eyes then. "No. I don't think so."

He'd always been able to move quickly. That too was a benefit of being the youngest. The moment the taxi swerved into the curb, he had her in his arms. "Since we're never going to date, then there's surely no harm in this."

He kissed her then. Later, there'd be time to wonder about the whys. Because he wanted to prove that what he'd experienced in the alley hadn't been just an adrenaline rush? Because he simply had to?

Whatever they were, the whys vanished the moment her flavor seeped into him. She was sinfully sweet. Soft and yet strong. And once more he was stunned at how quickly his need could spring to a boil. And she was with him all the way. Her fingers were gripping his shoulders, her body shuddering against his. She didn't hold back, didn't seem to believe in it.

He managed to pull away just before the blood drained completely from his head. She looked as stunned as he felt.

"The Potter Building," announced the taxi driver.

For a moment they stared at each other without speaking. And damn if he didn't admire that she was able to speak first.

"Why did you do that?"

"To give you something to think about. Forbidden fruit is always irresistible."

She opened her mouth, then shut it before she tried again. "You're..."

Sam grinned at her as he planted another quick kiss on her lips. "Yeah, I am."

IT WAS ONLY AFTER he'd seen her safely into the elevator that Sam gave the taxi driver another twenty. "We're just going to wait here for a while. If you see a green van or a thin guy in a gray T-shirt, black jeans and a beard, there's another twenty in it for you."

He waited for the driver to pocket the bill before he pulled out his cell phone. On the third ring, Luis picked up. "Yeah, boss?"

"What's Rabaut doing?"

"His limo got back to the club about half an hour ago. Tyrone's in the alley and can see him moving around in his apartment."

"Leave Tyrone in the alley and let him know you've got another job. He'll have to keep his eye on the front of the club too just in case Rabaut leaves. I want you to come down to the Potter Building. If the lady lawyer that Rabaut hooked up with this morning leaves, you're to keep her under close surveillance and let me know immediately. Okay?"

"Sure, boss. I'll be down there in fifteen minutes."

Sam settled back in the seat and closed his eyes. He wasn't sure what was going on, but he was going to figure it out. For the moment, he was just damn glad that for the first time all day, his fingers weren't tingling.

AS THE ELEVATOR SHOT UPWARD to the fortieth floor, the knot of apprehension in A.J.'s stomach grew. Not because of Sam. She was going to put him and his kisses out of her mind. She had plenty of other things to worry about other than a tall, dark, handsome stranger who could kiss like a dream and make her want...

Something she couldn't have. Forbidden fruit.

Well, she was a very disciplined person. She'd always been able to resist temptation when it stood in the way of something she wanted.

The problem was she wanted—

Stubbornly, she pushed Sam Romano out of her mind and concentrated on the only other occupant of the elevator, a young man in his late teens. She'd heard him ask one of the doormen for the floor number of Hancock, Potter and King. And he'd been staring at her ever since the doors had slid shut.

He certainly didn't fit the profile of the usual client of the firm. The long shaggy blond hair and the rings piercing his eyebrow and lower lip told her that he wasn't a summer intern either. Uncle Jamison would never have allowed it.

"Is there something wrong?" she asked. "Do I have a hole in my stocking?"

His gaze flew from her legs to her face. For a second he looked startled, almost as if she'd sprung him from a trance.

Then for the first time, she glanced over her shoulder to check herself out in the mirrors that lined the back wall of the elevator. She'd made a quick stop in the ladies' room to repair what she could of the damage done by racing through the streets in eighty-degree heat.

Suddenly, her gaze locked on the skirt. It was a lot shorter than it had looked in the apartment that morning. The tops of her thigh-high stockings were showing. How in the world—?

Grabbing the hem of the skirt with both hands, she tugged it until she felt the waistband ease down. Neither Samantha nor Claire had told her that the skirt had a tendency to hike up. She frowned at her image in the mirror. It had to be her hips. Everything she ate made a beeline for them. Mentally, she made a note to lengthen her kickboxing workout.

A long, low whistle had her glancing back at the young man. He'd hooked his thumbs into the pockets of his jeans and leaned back against the brass railing that lined the walls of the car. His face had settled into a smile that fell just short of a sneer. "Nothing's wrong that I can see. You look...hot. You wanna do something tonight?"

The attitude and the tough talk contrasted with the hint of fear she saw in his eyes. "Thanks. I *am* hot—hard not to be in this heat, but I don't suppose you mean it quite that way. And I have to meet with a client tonight." A client and Sam.

Never mind Sam! She focused her attention on the young man standing in front of her. "Do you have business with Hancock, Potter and King?"

"My Dad...I mean...I got an appointment with the Potter guy. You know anything about him?"

"Rodney or Jamison?" she asked.

"The one that's the head honcho."

"That'd be Jamison. He's my uncle. And I'm the other Potter—A.J." She held out her hand.

He hesitated for a minute, then grasped it. "I'm Parker. Parker Ellis Chase the Third. You can call me Park."

A.J.'s brows shot up and questions flooded into her mind. The name had rung an instant bell. Parker Ellis Chase was one of the firm's biggest clients, and Rodney had just been invited to work on the file. If this was the son and heir—no, he had to be the grandson—he was certainly in full rebellion.

Still holding her hand, he tried for a sneer again. "Does your uncle know any judges he can buy off?"

"Uncle Jamison doesn't buy off judges."

The boy shrugged, but she saw the fear flash into his eyes again.

"You're in trouble?"

"Just robbery. My dad had to fly back from Japan."

A.J. had to stifle her curiosity when the doors slid open. Her cousin Rodney rose from the corner of the receptionist's desk and strode toward her, a wide satisfied grin on his face. "Dad wants to see you ASAP."

"You in trouble?" Park asked as he dropped her hand and clenched both of his into fists.

"No. Not yet." She stepped in between him and her cousin. "I was detained by a new client."

"This him?" Rodney asked looking Park up and then down. "A dog, a hit-and-run victim, and now this. It figures. You're never going to impress the executive board by volunteering to take on pro bono work."

"Let me introduce you," A.J. said. "Meet Parker Ellis Chase the Third. He has an appointment with your father."

While the red flooded Rodney's face, A.J. took Park's arm and drew him to the glass doors behind the receptionist's desk. "My uncle's office is at the end of the hall to your left. His secretary will make you comfortable."

"I suppose you're very pleased with yourself," Rodney said as soon as the boy disappeared down the hall.

Walking back to him, she pitched her voice low. "No. I like that young man, and you insulted him."

His eyes narrowed. "You set me up. You told me he was your new client."

"No. I merely said a new client had delayed me. You jumped to the conclusion that I was referring to Parker."

"Whatever." Rodney pushed past her and pulled open the glass doors. "It won't be a problem anyway. I'll mend fences soon enough when I handle his case. He's due in court this afternoon."

She studied her cousin's retreating back for a moment. He'd resented her from the first moment her aunt and uncle had taken her in when she was seven. It had been a case of intense sibling rivalry at first sight.

And it had never worn off. Five years her senior, he had a four-year head start on her at the law firm and a father who not only handed out cases, but who could and would make him a partner in another year. Yet he seemed to hate her even more since she'd joined on at Hancock, Potter and King.

Maybe it was time she just flat out asked him why. She'd taken three steps after him when the receptionist said, "Ms. Potter? I have a call for you."

A.J. whirled back to take the phone. "A. J. Potter," she said into it.

"Just checking."

She recognized Sam's voice at once. "Checking what?"

"To see if your voice sounds the same on the phone as it does in person."

His did. Deep and low, it vibrated through her right to her toes.

"And to see if you made it up to the office without anyone mugging you."

"Of course I did. The building has security." She edged her hip onto the corner of the receptionist's desk.

"Just wanted to make sure. Besides, I'm not used to leaving my dates with doormen. I prefer to escort them right to the door."

"We weren't on a date, Romano."

The long sigh on the other end of the line had her biting back a grin.

"You know, I had just about convinced myself that your name had to be something sweet like Angela or Amy. But maybe I was on the right track with those tougher names. Maybe you're an Adrian or an Agatha or Agnes?"

She couldn't prevent a laugh from escaping.

"Look at it this way, counselor. You have to admit that our little...interlude this morning had at least some characteristics of a date."

"You must have a very strange date life."

"We walked, we talked," he continued. "Okay, make that

a run. But we had a bite to eat, I delivered you to your door in a taxi, and then I kissed you."

A.J. found she had to focus very hard not to let the memory of that kiss bring all of the sensations flooding back into her system.

"And you kissed me back."

She found the strength to hold up a finger. "Number one, we weren't on a date, and number two—"

"A.J."

She glanced up to see her uncle standing in the open doorway flanked by Rodney and a tall, distinguished-looking gray-haired man she recognized from magazine covers as Parker Ellis Chase the Second. Park's dad. "I've got to go," she said as she handed the phone back to the receptionist.

There were three beats of silence while the three men stared at her. Her uncle was glaring at her as if she'd committed some fatal social error.

Oops. Keeping her gaze steady on all three of them, she slid off the corner of the desk, pinching the fabric of the skirt and tugging it down as surreptitiously as she could. The waistband did its telltale slide. "Yes, sir?"

"This way," her uncle said. Then turning on his heel, he led them all in a parade back to his office.

It was not going to be good news. A.J. could feel it right down to her toes.

4

AS SHE SANK INTO A CHAIR at the far end of her uncle's desk, A.J. felt like a child who'd been summoned into the principal's office. He'd asked the Chases, father and son, as well as Rodney to wait outside for a moment. And now all he was doing was intimidating her further by silently sorting through the stack of papers his secretary had handed to him. She shifted her attention to the framed portraits lining the wall behind his desk—all Potters, all partners in the firm and all male. Rodney's would no doubt join the group next year.

And so would hers—eventually. She would see to that no matter what it took. Stifling her impatience, she folded her hands tightly in her lap and waited.

Uncle Jamison rarely spoke to her at home or at work. He was a man of serious demeanor and very few words, a flaw her aunt more than made up for. Growing up in his house, A.J. could count on one hand the number of times he'd given her advice. The last time had been to suggest she take some time off and enjoy herself rather than go to law school. When she'd ignored him and entered Harvard Law School anyway, he'd told her that he expected her to work at Hancock, Potter and King when she graduated. Not that she was wanted there. No, that was never even implied. His exact words were— "It would be a public embarrassment to the firm if you sought employment elsewhere."

"You're enjoying your new apartment?"

A.J. very nearly glanced over her shoulder to see who her

uncle could possibly be talking to. But she knew that no one had entered the room. "It's fine. My roommates are great. The neighbors are a little...unusual. Nice though."

The noise her uncle made in reply was hard to interpret and she studied him through narrowed eyes. Was he ill? The few times she'd been summoned to his office before, there'd been a problem. The last time was when she'd started to do pro bono work, accepting cases that the Public Defender's office wasn't able to handle. He'd at least been fair that day, and she'd won her case with him by pointing out the goodwill it would earn for the firm. She'd also promised him that her work for the firm wouldn't suffer.

That had been the end of it. He'd never questioned her again about any outside work she'd done, nor were any of the cases she'd handled ever brought up at the monthly meeting, not even when she'd been successful.

"As you're probably aware, the firm's golf outing is tomorrow."

A.J. was very much aware of it. Hancock, Potter and King took its golf seriously. Firm members would hit the links early and play hard and head back to the city. Since the exclusive country club in Westchester where they held their outing didn't allow women on the course until after 4:00 p.m., she'd been looking forward to a day off.

"Your aunt will be hosting a cocktail party tomorrow after the outing. She wants you to be there. She's even made an appointment at her salon for you."

A.J. drew in a breath. "I don't think I—"

"I'd like you to be there. I received a call from a prospective client this morning. He could produce quite a bit of revenue for the firm, and he wanted to meet all of the Potters who worked for the firm. They're a family company and they are interested in having a family represent them." Jamison cleared his throat. "They mentioned seeing you on TV this morning in a news clip."

"All right. I'll be there. The usual time—five to seven?"

Her uncle nodded, then finally took his chair and said, "I also received a phone call from Pierre Rabaut this morning. He's transferring all of his business to our firm, and he wants you to handle it."

A.J. stared at him.

"He told me how you saved his life, as well as how you offered to handle matters for him when he gave his statement to the police. He also told me that I was lucky to have an attorney working here with such a fine legal mind and a true generosity of spirit."

A.J. couldn't find her voice. Pierre hadn't mentioned any of this to her.

Uncle Jamison cleared his throat. "Good work."

She just barely kept her jaw from dropping open. "Thank you."

"On a different topic—what do you know about Judge Stanton?"

"She's known as the hanging judge down at the Public Defender's office."

"And what is your take on her?"

A.J. blinked. First a compliment and now he was asking her opinion? Her uncle had never done either one before. She shot a quick glance at her skirt. It had to be working. Then meeting her uncle's eyes, she said, "Judge Stanton prides herself on being evenhanded. She doesn't believe that the way to rid this city of crime is to coddle the more economically deprived defendants. But she's very careful not to favor the rich simply because they have more money."

Her uncle nodded. "You won your last case in front of her."

For the second time in as many minutes, A.J. struggled to keep her jaw from dropping.

"I've kept track of your trial work. I need to know about Stanton because Mr. Chase's son is scheduled to appear in front of her at 3:00 p.m. I couldn't get a postponement."

"She doesn't give them easily."

"The boy's in serious trouble this time. He's had two other run-ins with the law. Mr. Chase has some influence, and I was able to get the boy off with probation both times. This time his credit line has run out. A.D.A. Collins refused to cut a deal. You're going to have your work cut out for you."

"My work..."

His uncle gave her a thin smile. "Young Mr. Chase is adamant. You're the Potter he wants representing him in court this afternoon. And it just might work. When Judge Stanton looks at you, she won't see the same connotation of money and influence she sees when she looks at me." He shoved a file across his desk as he rose. "You have about two hours to meet with your clients and to prepare."

IT WAS AT SOME POINT during the time that the assistant district attorney was summing up his case against Parker Ellis Chase the Third that A.J. felt the tingling sensation at the back of her neck. Even before she turned, she was sure it was Sam. And when her eyes met his briefly across the several empty rows of seats in the courtroom, she told herself that it wasn't pleasure she felt. She was merely surprised to see him.

"And what do you have to say on behalf of your client, Ms. Potter?"

Dragging her attention back to the proceedings, A.J. felt anything but prepared as she rose to her feet in front of Judge Stanton. The woman was pulling on her earring, and that was a very bad sign.

The case that A.D.A. Collins had made was admirable. He was willing to have the kid bound over to trial as a juvenile, but he wanted him to do some time. After all, two rulings of probation hadn't done anything to rehabilitate him. What guarantee was there that it would do any good this time?

As she made her own case, A.J. could hear the flaws in it. And the judge could clearly see the problem. The two Chases sitting in front of her presented anything but the picture of a solid family. The mother who had custody was out of the country. The father was glancing at his watch or his vibrating pager every few moments, and the son sat sullen and scared at his side.

If she'd been in Judge Stanton's place, she would have seen *repeat offender* written all over Park's face. Sending him home to his mother's empty apartment while his father hopped the next plane back to Japan was not going to solve anything. As she spoke, she concentrated on convincing the judge of exactly that.

"Ms. Potter, you're a bright young attorney. You handled yourself well in the Billings case a few months back. But you seem to be telling me that young Mr. Chase is very likely to steal again if I release him. And the fact that his father is willing to make restitution doesn't erase the crime. Am I correct?"

"I'm afraid so, your Honor. That's why I'm not recommending that young Mr. Chase be given probation and released into his parents' care this time."

Judge Stanton stopped pulling at her earring and frowned. "You're not?"

A.J. drew in a deep breath. "I have a different suggestion."

"If the defense is going to suggest community service," Collins said, "I'll have to object. Without supervision, he won't show up and we'll be back here in a week."

"Ms. Potter?" Judge Stanton asked.

"I agree. He probably won't. His mother is out of the country and his father will be as soon as this hearing is over. That's why if your Honor would be willing, I can make arrangements for Park to be placed in Father Danielli's home for boys down in Soho. There he will have the opportunity to do community service and he will be supervised."

Judge Stanton's eyes narrowed. "There's a waiting list at Father Danielli's. I've got two young men on it right now."

"I can get him in, your Honor," A.J. said. "I spoke with Father Danielli just before I came to court."

For a moment, there was silence in the courtroom. A.J. held her breath and crossed her fingers behind her back. Persuading Father Danielli to take Park in had been a breeze compared to the effort she'd put into convincing the two Chases. In the end, Chase Senior had agreed because he had a meeting to attend, and Park had agreed because for some reason he seemed to trust her.

"Stand up, young man." Judge Stanton studied him for a moment. "If I agree to your attorney's suggestion, will you do your part?"

"Your Honor, my son—" Parker Chase Senior began.

"I don't believe I addressed you, sir. Young man, will you stay at the home and obey the rules?"

A.J. put a hand on Park's arm.

"Yes, ma'am," said Park.

"Father Danielli will get you a job. You think you can hold down a job?"

"I'll try, ma'am."

That seemed to satisfy her more than Park's first reply had. She pointed a finger at him. "See to it that you do. You should feel lucky that I am familiar with Father Danielli and the work that he does. Doubly lucky because your attorney has enough pull with him to get you in. Otherwise, the results of the hearing would be very different. The next time I see you here, you're going to trial and you'll do time."

She shifted her finger towards A.J. "I want a weekly report, Ms. Potter. You'll see to it that I get one."

"Yes, your Honor."

"Next case."

SAM WATCHED the two Chases and A.J. walk down the steps of the courthouse. He was almost getting used to the feeling—the gnawing ache in his gut that bordered on pain—that hit him whenever he saw her. Almost. He'd never experienced anything quite like it before.

A smart man would keep his distance. But it wasn't in his nature to walk away from unanswered questions, and he had a lot of them where A.J. was concerned. From what kind of a lawyer she was to what she liked on her toast in the morning. And more.

At least one of his questions had been answered. A. J. Potter was a damn good trial attorney.

As a P.I., he'd spent enough time in courtrooms to appreciate a lawyer who knew how to play the judge just right. And A.J. had done just that. The assistant DA had told her as much, albeit grudgingly, as they'd walked down the aisle together. Of course, he'd also warned her that the Chase kid would be back in court within the month.

Both Chases seemed subdued at the moment. The older one was saying something to A.J. as he held the door of a taxi open for his son.

Taking a quick scan of the courthouse steps, Sam spotted Luis standing with a group of people who looked to be jurors on a break. The kid was getting better at keeping a discreet distance when he was tailing someone. Sam turned his attention to the street. It was nearly five, and there was no sign of Pierre's limo in front of Emile's Café.

As if on cue, a sleek black limousine pulled up behind the Chases' taxi just as it shot away from the curb. Sam had time to recognize Pierre's driver as he circled around the hood to open the door. He and A.J. had both started toward the limo when the green van pulled up alongside it and another limo pulled up behind it. Two men, the size of linebackers, climbed out of the limo. The bearded guy jumped out of the van and headed in A.J.'s direction.

Sam broke into a dead run.

"Luis!" He was barely able to shout before one of the linemen stepped into his path. Sam went in low. Out of the corner of his eye he saw A.J. swing her purse. Then he rammed into the large man like a battering ram. It felt as if he'd just run full tilt into a brick wall, but the momentum sent them both tumbling onto the cement sidewalk. A second later, his body empty of breath, Sam looked up to see Luis fasten himself on top of the bearded man. Pierre's driver was rolling on the ground with the other linebacker.

As Sam scrambled to his feet, he saw A.J. aim a kick into the bearded man's groin. Racing forward, he made a grab for A.J.'s hand, but he gripped only air before he was grabbed from behind, lifted off his feet and thrown to the sidewalk. Pain burning through him, he rolled across the cement as a huge foot barely missed his face.

The muffled scream had him twisting around, and he saw that it was the bearded man clutching his head and sagging against the side of the limo. A.J. was winding up, purse in hand, for another shot.

"Run," he yelled at A.J. Then twisting again, he scissored his legs around one of his opponent's and held on for the ride as the big man tried to shake him loose.

Pain slammed through him each time his bones connected with cement, but he held on. A crowd had begun to gather, but no one was rushing forward.

Smart, Sam thought. They could see that the big guy was hammering him. Pierre's driver was serving as a punching bag for the other big man, and through blurred vision, Sam saw Luis fly through the air.

Releasing his own half of the defensive line, Sam rolled clear of the man's size fifteen shoe and leapt to his feet. One glance around told him he had about five seconds to figure out how to play it.

Pierre was safe, standing at the side of his limo, but a seventy-year-old man, no matter how fit, was not going to be much help. Luis was spread-eagled on the ground. Pierre's bodyguard had his opponent in a hammerlock. The one Sam had just shaken loose was lunging toward him again with A.J. in hot pursuit. It was the thin bearded guy pushing himself away from the limo toward A.J. that decided it for Sam. He had to get A.J. out of there.

Rolling forward to the balls of his feet, he locked his gaze on the man barreling toward him. At the very last moment, he dodged to the right then smashed his fist into the man's mouth. Pain sang up his arm. Ignoring it, he brought his knee up hard and sent the big guy staggering back. Dodging to the left, Sam dashed past him towards A.J.

"Run," he managed, though the word was more a gasp than a sound. Then grabbing her hand to make sure she did, he pivoted and dragged her with him.

"Pierre," she said. "We shouldn't...leave him."

"He's got his driver," Sam answered. The moment he had A.J. at a safe distance, he would go back.

When he reached the corner, he glanced back just in time to see the two big guys grab a struggling Pierre and drag him toward the second limousine. Pierre's driver and Luis lay prone on the sidewalk.

"They're kidnapping Pierre," A.J. said as she raced past him. Even as he snatched hold of her hand and kept pace, the two men shoved Pierre into the back seat. One climbed in after him and the other slid into the driver's seat. A second later, the limo screeched away from the curb and made a U-turn. The green van nearly hit a pedestrian when it followed. Dragging in air, Sam forced himself to run faster. In some part of his mind, he was aware that a crowd had formed around the two prone men and that a reporter with a video camera had started to film the scene. He also heard the sound of sirens coming closer. But he kept his attention focused on the limo, willing it to slow at the first intersection.

It didn't.

"Faster," he said to A.J. as he pushed himself into a sprint. She kept up with him. But they were still a good twenty yards away when the limo, tires squealing, careened around the corner and shot out of sight. The van followed two car lengths behind. Twenty seconds later, when they reached the intersection, both vehicles had disappeared.

For a moment, they stood there, hands clasped, breathing hard. When Sam glanced back at the courthouse, he saw that Pierre's driver had gotten to his feet. And Luis was sitting up.

"AYE 4220." A.J. pulled out her Palm Pilot and pressed in the numbers. "That's the limo. And JFM 3712 is the van."

It was a moment before he registered what she'd said. Then he grabbed her and swung her around. Pain shot through his ribs, but he barely felt it. "You got the license plates. Damn, but you're good!"

AN HOUR LATER, A.J. and Sam finished reporting what had happened to one of the detectives who'd been called to the scene by two uniformed officers.

"So what do you plan to do about it?" she said as he tucked his notebook into his pocket.

"We've put out an APB on the green van and the limo with

the license plate you gave us," the detective said. "We have descriptions of all three men, and we'll make sure the media keeps a lid on it. Kidnappers usually want something. If they get in touch with you, call me."

"So all we can do is wait? Pierre's an old man," she said.

"We're doing everything we can," the detective said.

"He's right. All we can do right now is wait. And remember that Pierre is a lot tougher than he looks," Sam said as the detective walked to his car.

She would have argued. She whirled on him ready to do just that, but one look at Sam's face stopped her. He had a nasty scrape on one cheekbone and a split and swollen lip, but it was his eyes that told her whatever fears she had for Pierre, his were greater. "You're right. He is tough," she said instead. She slipped her hand into his and felt his fingers squeeze hard on hers.

"I thought he'd be all right. I was sure that his driver and Luis could handle those two men for a few minutes. Dammit."

She laid her free hand on his cheek. "We'll find him. We'll get him back."

"Yeah." Hearing her say it helped him to believe it. Sam drew in a deep breath and let it out. The emotions running through him were clouding his ability to think clearly. And he couldn't afford that. He needed to be objective.

"You look awful," she said. "Your lip might need stitches."

"Nah. It just needs some ice." He managed a grin, then winced. "I was thinking you might play nurse. All we have to decide is your place or mine."

Her eyes flew to his in an instant. "You can't possibly be thinking of..."

His voice turned low. "Of making love to you?" He smiled

more carefully this time. "Yeah, on some level, I'm pretty much thinking about it all the time."

She ignored the long, slow tumble her heart took. "Well, stop. You ought to be thinking about going to an emergency room. That bozo nearly killed you."

He raised both hands, palms out. "Before you swing that purse at me, I was just thinking we both need to get cleaned up. And I'm not going to let you out of my sight until I figure out what in hell is going on here. So, your place or mine?"

He was still angry. Beneath the humor and the banter, she could sense the ripe fury. And the fear. Because she could relate to both emotions, she said, "My place. I have a first-aid kit. And it isn't a date."

"Agreed." He grinned and winced again. "I want our first date to be special. I have a place I'm going to take you where the view of Manhattan is spectacular. We can dance under the stars and no one will disturb us." He ran a finger along her jawline. "And then we'll make love for a very long time."

She didn't say a word. She wasn't sure she could. They were just words, simple straightforward, nothing flowery. But when Sam said them, she wanted them to be true. He touched only her face, and yet he might as well have been touching all of her. She wanted him to touch all of her.

"Think about it," he said as he brushed a quick kiss on her mouth.

A.J. knew she wasn't going to have much choice.

ANY HOPE SHE HAD of sneaking Sam into her apartment unnoticed was completely banished as soon as she entered the lobby. Cleo and Mrs. Higgenbotham, who was dressed in a pink caftan so bright it made A.J. squint, were totally engrossed in the scene taking place beneath the skylight. There, Franco in a short red tunic and tights, was down on his knees, his face raised toward the skylight, one hand slowly reaching upward.

"A horse! A hooooorse! My kingdom for a hoooorse!"

In the dramatic moment of silence that followed, A.J. squeezed Sam's hand and spoke in a tone only he could hear. "Relax. I promise you we're not at Bellevue."

"And the guy with the equestrian fetish is...?"

"Franco Rossi, my doorman, and the woman is my neighbor Heloise Higgenbotham. She owns Cleo."

As if on cue, Mrs. Higgenbotham began to clap enthusiastically, setting all of her bracelets jangling. "Bravo! Bravo! Franco, I look at you, and I truly see Henry the Fifth."

Franco leapt to his feet. "Well, the trick will be not to blink while you're looking! In a thirty-second commercial, I'll probably be on screen for two at the most. If I'm lucky."

"You got the part!" Drawing Sam with her, A.J. hurried forward to give Franco a hug. "Congratulations!"

Quickly, she made the introductions, but Cleo ignored the formalities and began shamelessly licking Sam's free hand.

Mrs. Higgenbotham fluttered her eyelashes and murmured. "Oh my. Oh *my.* A.J., you should have warned me you were bringing home a gentleman caller. And such a strong, handsome one at that." Then she blinked and peered more closely at Sam. "You're hurt."

"I'll bet he cleans up well," Franco said as he circled slowly around Sam. Then, rubbing his hands together, he flashed A.J. a grin. "I approve. That skirt is on its way to creating its own urban legend. If I ever break up with Marlon, I'm absolutely going to have to borrow it."

"What skirt?" Mrs. Higgenbotham asked.

"The one A.J. is wearing. It's guaranteed to attract men," Franco explained. "And very attractive men at that. I suppose you're straight?"

"Yes," Sam said.

"That skirt looks very ordinary to me," Mrs. Higgenbotham said studying it closely. "I've seen one exactly like it at Bloomingdale's."

"Knockoffs," Franco explained with a wave of his hand. "That's the problem with the modern world. Nothing is unique anymore." Leaning down, he fingered the hem of A.J.'s skirt. "But this skirt is woven out of a special fiber that grows only on this island. Can't you smell it?"

"You want to drop the skirt?" Sam asked tersely.

"Sure. No problem," Franco said, raising both hands, palms out.

They'd never get upstairs if they didn't make their escape now. Keeping a tight grip on Sam's hand, A.J. began backing toward the elevator. Mrs. Higgenbotham and Cleo followed, stalking them step for step.

"I have just the thing for that lip. It's a special formula that I brought home from Paris the last time I was there."

"Thanks," Sam managed. "But A.J. is going to fix me up good as new."

"I'll just bet she will," Franco said, sending A.J. a wink.

"I'll let her borrow the ointment," Mrs. Higgenbotham insisted. "And you can tell me more about the skirt."

The elevator door was open, but A.J. stopped short of entering it. There was only one sure way to distract Mrs. H. "How did Cleo's appointment go? Did the past life regression therapy help?"

Mrs. Higgenbotham blinked. "Oh! Yes, it did. I nearly forgot...Dr. Fielding believes that poor Cleo has a lost love from her past life and she's desperately searching for him. That's why she's so...itchy, if you know what I mean."

Yes. A.J. did know. "Itch" was as good a word as any to describe the ever-deepening yearning that had been growing hotter and sharper during the taxi ride to her apartment. She'd been trying to analyze just what it was about Sam that was causing her to want to break all her rules and just throw caution to the winds. And she thought she'd figured it out.

It wasn't just his good looks or that killer smile or even the way he kissed her. No, it was more than that. It also had to do with his words and that intent way he had of looking at her as if he already knew things about her that she didn't know herself. All of it, the whole package, was making her...itch. Badly. In spite of all her work to become a true Potter, was she deep down just like her mother—irresistibly attracted to someone who was all wrong for her?

Mrs. Higgenbotham glanced at her watch. "I have an appointment at the kennel club. Dr. Fielding said it might help if Cleo looked at some pictures of the dogs we've selected as good breeding partners. She might recognize him, and then I could make the arrangements and speed the mating process along."

The mating process.

Mrs. Higgenbotham's phrase hung in the air as the door slid shut, leaving her alone with Sam in the elevator. She didn't dare look at him. But she couldn't prevent her head from turning. He was closer than she'd thought. One look into those dark, intent eyes, and she knew what he meant to do—what she wanted him to do.

"We came here to fix that scrape on your face and your lip, not to—"

"We'll get to all of that in the apartment." He shifted, trapping her against the back of the elevator. "I can't wait any longer to do this. I thought I could." He brushed his lips over hers. "I can't."

"Sam, I—" But the rest of what she was going to say slipped away when his lips brushed hers again very softly.

"Your pulse is skipping right here." She could feel it when he moved his lips to her throat. "It's so exciting."

"We really...shouldn't." The words were hard to push out

through a throat that felt as if it had been suddenly stuffed with cotton. "We should be thinking of how to find Pierre."

His eyes, steady and intent, met hers. "I have great powers of concentration. I'm pretty sure you do too, counselor. We can keep our minds on finding Pierre and still wonder what it would be like to make love with each other." His lips brushed hers again as he spoke. "Tell me. Haven't you wondered?"

A.J. gripped the handrail on the elevator wall behind her to steady herself. She suddenly felt winded, weak. When his mouth covered hers, it was like coming home. But it wasn't like any home she'd ever known. That was the last coherent thought that she was aware of before the flood of sensations took over. She could feel everything—the silkiness of his hair as her fingers threaded through it, each plane and angle of his body as it brushed against hers.

Want changed to need in the length of time it took his mouth to turn hot and hard on hers. She welcomed the demand and answered it. Need sprinted to desperation in the seconds it took him to draw back for an instant and change the angle of the kiss.

AS HE TOOK HER MOUTH AGAIN, he concentrated on going slowly. He wanted to draw the pleasure out for both of them. But he hadn't counted on the simple need he had to lose himself in her.

She felt so soft, so strong—and so right. Was that what had excitement and need building at a breakneck speed? He wanted to touch her, all of her. But he fastened his hands on the railing at her back to steady himself and drew back to nip at her lips instead. Her low, throaty moan was nearly his undoing. He didn't dare to touch her then. He wouldn't be able to stop.

Her lips were swollen, and in her violet eyes there was a hunger that matched what he was feeling.

He could have her. He could see her looking at him just this way when he drew her to the floor and mounted her. All he had to do was push the button that would stop the elevator. It would be wild and wonderful. The image that filled his mind had him gripping the railing behind her.

But he wanted more than a quick round of elevator sex with A.J. He wanted a lot more. That sudden realization stunned him. He eased himself back a step. It occurred to him that he was definitely in over his head. As the youngest of three brothers, it wasn't a new experience for him. What he needed to do was think about it a little and come up with a plan to handle it. Gently, he pulled A.J. against him and held her.

"What are we going to do about this?" she asked.

Sam laughed. "I had a pretty good plan going there—but I figured Franco and Cleo's mommy would have the same idea if the elevator suddenly stopped between floors."

"I would have let you. I would have enjoyed it. I've never done anything like that in my life. I never wanted to before."

With a groan, Sam rested his head against hers as he felt the blood drain out of it. "That's not something you should say to me when we're alone in an elevator."

"Sorry, but we've got a problem, and it helps me to get all of the information out there. I need to figure out why you have this effect on me."

Sam put all his effort into a grin. "Maybe it's the amazing way I kiss. We could give it another shot and test my theory."

The elevator door slid open, and A.J. pulled him with her into the hall.

"Take off your clothes."

Sam pulled A.J. to a stop and stared at the woman who

had a voice as deep and sexy as Lauren Bacall and who was blocking their way down the hall. She had short gray hair and a slim, toned body. That and the skin-tight exercise clothes she wore attested to regular workouts.

"I'm one of A.J.'s neighbors," Petra said. "I think you're just what I'm looking for."

Stepping in front of Sam, A.J. said, "He's not available, Petra."

"Every man is available for the right price," the woman drawled as she peered around A.J. "But before I make an offer, I need to see you with your clothes off. Are you available on Tuesdays?"

"I'm terribly sorry, but Sam is busy every day. I've just hired him to do some work for me."

"My dear, I don't have designs on him. I just want his body." Whipping a card out of the very tight space between the tank top and her breasts, Petra extended it to Sam, then began to circle him. "It's all for the sake of art. You have the most lovely biceps. But I really need to see if you have the right kind of butt."

Taking a quick side step, A.J. blocked Petra's view.

"Maybe later," Petra said as she backed into the elevator. "By the way, A.J., I slipped a letter under your door a while ago. It was delivered by special messenger and Franco asked me to bring it up."

The moment the elevator doors slid shut, A.J. turned to Sam and raised one hand. "Don't say a word."

"I was just going to say that you have the most interesting friends. And I like her. I actually like them all," he continued as he followed her down the hall. "But I do have a special place in my heart for someone who asks me to strip on sight."

"Petra asks every man she meets to strip on sight," A.J. said as she unlocked the door and led the way into the apartment. "The first time I met her I thought she was a talent agent for a male strip club. But she's a sculptor. At least that's the excuse she gives for having nude men parading around her apartment at all hours."

A.J. slipped out of her shoes, then scooped them up as she lifted the courier-delivered envelope off the floor. It contained a single sheet of paper, and as she read it, she frowned.

"Bad news?" Sam asked, moving toward her.

She handed it to him, and the words on it sent a chill down his spine.

"'You have something that belongs to me. I'll be in touch.'"

5

STANDING IN THE DOORWAY to the kitchen, Sam watched A.J. place wineglasses on a tray. Aside from calling Franco to see if he recalled anything particular about the man who'd delivered the letter, she hadn't said more than two words since she'd handed him the note.

Her courage constantly amazed him. Then he noticed her hand tremble just a little as she began to uncork the wine. Perhaps it was the tough outer shell she tried to put on that made her vulnerability even more appealing. One thing he knew for sure, he was frightened for her.

He'd phoned Tyrone and asked him to check out the delivery service. It was a long shot, but someone might be able to describe the person who'd paid for the delivery. And he wanted to make sure her apartment was safe without alarming her any further. But first...

"Talk to me, A.J. You don't have to handle this alone."

"I'm trying to convince myself that some crank sent it. What else could it be?"

"It could be the kidnappers. You were on TV this morning with Pierre. They might think he told you something about the necklace."

"But it isn't stolen."

"Someone besides me evidently believes that it was." He moved toward her and taking the wine bottle, poured her a glass. When she'd taken a sip, he said, "You know, I haven't thanked you yet for protecting my virtue with your friend Petra."

A.J. struggled with a smile. "I draw the line at providing her with naked men."

"Well, that's good to know. You also told her you'd hired me. What do you have in mind?"

"I want you to help me find Pierre. I don't think we should just sit around and wait for the kidnappers to call."

Sam took her free hand in his. "That's what you have to do sometimes. One of the toughest parts of being a P.I. is the waiting. And kidnappers know that. They'll make us wait, knowing that we'll just get more worried, more desperate. And I don't think they'll hurt Pierre. Not until they get their hands on what they want. We just have to be patient."

"I'm not." She met his eyes then, and the moment she did, her expression changed. "I...oh, I'm so sorry. I completely forgot why we came here. Your face. I'll get the first-aid kit."

Sam waited until she'd disappeared into the hallway before he grabbed the opportunity to look around. Taking the stairs two at a time, he glanced around the loft. It was clear. Then he returned to the first floor and moved down the hall. Opening the door to his left, he quickly checked the closet and the windows. No fire escape, nothing under the bed. The next room was also empty.

He knew the moment he entered the third that it was A.J.'s. Her scent surrounded him. A sly-looking auburn-haired stuffed fox sat in a rocking chair and geraniums overflowed from pots lined up along the windowsill. Above the bed hung a painting of poppies, a bright explosion in shades of red and pink.

They made him think of A.J. The pink reminded him of her sweetness and generosity, the red of that energy and passion he'd sensed in her from the beginning—all the more alluring because she tried so hard to hold it in check.

"What are you doing in here?"

He turned to find A.J. standing in the doorway.

"My job," he said. "I wanted to make certain there aren't any surprise visitors waiting to jump you."

"What on earth are you talking about?" Then she frowned. "Did those bullies give you a concussion?"

"No. Just one terrific headache. You got any aspirin in that first-aid kit?"

Opening it up, she gestured for him to sit down on the bed. Then she set the kit down next to him and began to stroke his cheek with a damp cloth.

"Ouch. What have you got on that?" Sam asked.

"Antiseptic soap," she said as she folded the cloth over and then began to stroke his cheek with it again. "Better?"

"Much."

A.J. put all her effort into concentrating on her job. But it was hard. He was so close that his scent was all she could breathe. Sunshine and sweat and something else that was very dark and male. There was something very intimate in rubbing the cloth across his face.

"Why are you so fixated on the notion that I'm in some kind of danger?" she asked to get her mind off the fact that he was sitting on her bed.

"Fixated? That bearded man made a beeline for you the minute he stepped out of his van. In the P.I. business we call it looking at the bare hard facts."

Another bare hard fact was that something was happening to her legs. They felt weak, just as they had when she'd run down that alley this morning. Sam was so close. Putting the cloth down, she reached for the ointment and began to apply it. "Does this feel all right?"

"Fine."

Rubbing her fingers over his face felt more than fine to her. And it was a mistake to look into his eyes. They were very calm, very close and very intent. She could see herself in them—trapped. Deep inside, she could feel her defenses melting and seeping away. His mouth was close too. His breath whispered on her skin. It would be so easy to lean closer, to taste. And he was watching her, waiting for her to make that small move. And she wanted to make it. She wanted him—just as she'd wanted him in the elevator. More than anything.

But she was afraid.

And how could she be thinking of making love to Sam Romano when they should be thinking about rescuing Pierre?

"I—" Somehow she found the strength to take a step back. "I can't." She took three quick backward steps toward the door. "We can't. I'm going to get that wine. And then you can go. You've got to find Pierre."

HE WAS GOING TO NEED a long drink of that wine, Sam thought. It had been sheer torture to have her hands on his face and know that if he made a move he could have had those hands on his body. He could have had her on the bed right then and there. He would have if she hadn't looked so vulnerable. No, for a moment there, it was fear he'd seen in her eyes. Of him or herself, he wasn't sure. Carefully, he packed the supplies back into the first-aid kit. He would wait until she was ready.

But he wasn't going to leave her. She might not want to accept it, but whoever had wanted Pierre had wanted A.J. too. Fear and frustration knotted in his stomach. Every time he thought about his godfather...

He pressed his fingers to his eyes. He couldn't let the fear get to him. Pierre would be all right. He was clever, and he'd gotten himself out of tight spots before. *Always do the unexpected.* A man with a motto like that would have a few tricks up his sleeve to handle kidnappers. He had to believe that.

In the meantime, he would protect A.J. Until Pierre was found and they'd straightened this whole mess out, he was going to find a way to be with her twenty-four/seven.

Rising, he began to pace back and forth in the bedroom. The more he thought about it, the more he was convinced that the kidnappers had wanted to take her too. And she might know something, something that Pierre told her that she wasn't even aware of. His glance fell on a picture framed on her nightstand. Lifting it, he took a closer look. A strikingly handsome man who looked to be in his late twenties stared back at him. He had blond hair, a mile-wide smile, and he was standing at the wheel of a sailboat.

Sam had never known that jealousy could slice to the quick—not until he read the inscription.

"To Arianna, with all my love."

A.J. POURED WINE, but it was only as she lifted the glasses that she noticed her hand was shaking. Her hands never shook. And she was pretty sure it wasn't Sam's theory that she'd almost been kidnapped along with Pierre that was bothering her. She just couldn't decide what to do about Sam Romano. And she had a feeling her time was running out.

Good lord, she thought as she took a sip of the wine. She was as bad as Cleo—wanting someone who was all wrong for her. And she didn't doubt in the least that Sam thought of her the same way. His father had fallen for someone from a different world and had been very unhappy. Surely Sam wouldn't want to repeat his father's mistake any more than she wanted to repeat her mother's.

"About your idea of hiring me to find Pierre..."

She glanced up at him.

"I've got a better idea. Why don't we work together as partners—like Dr. Watson and Sherlock Holmes?" He raised two fingers. "I can think of two good reasons. Number one,

I'm beginning to think I'm too close to the case. I could use a second set of eyes and a sharp mind to help me figure out what's going on."

She studied him for a minute. "And number two?"

"You're a smart attorney. When we find Pierre, he's going to need your advice."

Her eyes narrowed. "You'd make a pretty good attorney yourself."

"Nah. I like catching the bad guys too much." Crossing to her, he picked up her free hand and placed it over the other one holding the wineglass. "Hold it in both hands. That's what I do when my hands shake."

She did as he told her and bit back a smile. "I can't imagine your hands shaking."

"Everyone gets scared. It doesn't mean you're a coward. It just means you're smart. I'm not going to let anything happen to you."

He was kind, she thought as she continued to study him. And it moved her more deeply than it should have.

He touched his glass against hers, then when she'd taken a swallow, he said, "To our new partnership."

A.J. studied him over the rim of her glass. "Not so fast. What's the real reason you want me to be your Watson, Sherlock?"

Sam threw back his head and laughed. "Because I can't put anything over on you. I meant it when I said I wanted that razor-sharp mind of yours."

"And?"

His expression sobered. "Until Pierre is found and this mess is straightened, I'm not going to let you out of my sight unless Luis or Tyrone is taking my place."

"Sam, I—"

"Why don't we discuss it over dinner? I know this really great restaurant. Maybe I mentioned it?"

She set her wineglass down and folded her arms in front of her. "If I agree to this, our partnership will be strictly business. I am not going out with you on a date. And there are some other ground rules we'll have to lay down."

"Absolutely. Rule number one, we have to have some brain food. It's been a long time since that hot dog. I'll fix you dinner here and that will allow us to get to rule number two—we get to know each other better. Partners should know each other, don't you think?"

A.J. smiled slowly. "What I think is that you won't be able to find enough food in this apartment to make anything resembling a dinner."

"You're on." Sam opened the refrigerator and swore.

She managed not to laugh as she peered over his shoulder. Aside from the wine and a case of bottled water, there was a pathetic-looking bunch of broccoli, a small wedge of cheese and three eggs.

"Okay, this is going to be a challenge, but a Romano doesn't give up."

He didn't. And he'd done this kind of thing before. A.J. could tell by the competent way he assembled a bowl, a frying pan and especially by the careful way he selected just the right knife from the block.

Intrigued, she settled herself on a stool at the counter to watch. In seconds, he peeled an onion he'd found in a hanging basket and began to chop it. "You're really good at that."

Without pausing or even hesitating in the swift, clean strokes he was making with the knife, Sam met her eyes. "All the Romanos can cook. We were practically raised in a hotel kitchen—Henry's Place in the East Sixties. It was either learn to cook or wash dishes. My oldest brother Tony runs the place now with some help from my cousin Lucy. Grace wants to follow in my cousin Nick's footsteps and go to law school."

"It sounds like fun—growing up in a big family like that."

The coziness, the shared laughter—they were what she'd always dreamed of as a child.

"It depends on whether or not hysteria and chaos fit your definition of fun. And there's not a lot of privacy. Everybody knows your business. So," he continued as he broke eggs into a bowl, "what about you? Why don't you cook?"

A.J. ran her finger around the top of her wineglass. "My Aunt Margery has a French chef. He doesn't allow anyone in the kitchen. Not that a Potter would go there."

"Sounds dull. What about before that? You didn't always live with your aunt and uncle."

"No." She rarely allowed herself to think of the time between her parents' deaths and the day that her Uncle Jamison came to take her home. She met Sam's eyes and saw the patience there. "My parents owned a charter boat business in the Caribbean. After they died in a boating accident, I was put in foster care for a while. Until I was seven. There wasn't a lot of food to cook in those homes."

For a moment, neither one of them spoke as Sam poured eggs into a skillet and began to gently swish them around in the pan. "You must have been very grateful to your aunt and uncle for taking you in."

There was understanding and kindness in the look that he sent her. She let out a breath she hadn't known she was holding. "Yes. I promised myself that day that I would make them proud of me."

Sam folded the eggs over with a quick snap of his wrist and slipped them deftly onto a plate. Placing the plate on the table, he said, "Eat."

It wasn't until the flavors exploded on her tongue that A.J. realized she was starving.

SAM WATCHED HER EAT the last mouthful of omelet. She ate with the same focus, the same energy she did everything else. Then she set down her fork, folded her napkin and aligned it very precisely beside the plate. He wondered if she would bring those same qualities to her lovemaking. He wasn't sure how long he would be able to prevent himself from finding out.

Finally she glanced up at him. "That was wonderful. But now I really think we should get to the ground rules."

Reining in his thoughts, he managed a smile. "I'm not really good at following rules, Arianna."

"You'll have to try—" She broke off to stare at him. "How did you—?"

"Good detective work. I saw the picture on your nightstand. Who's the guy?" He was pretty sure he wasn't one of the disastrous dates that had caused her to give up dating. A woman wasn't likely to keep a reminder of one of them in a place where she could see it waking and sleeping.

"My father."

He saw the flash of pain, and, in response, he felt guilt mixed with relief. He reached for her hand.

"He gave the picture to my mother. It's the only thing I have of them. I was named after my mother. That's why I changed my name."

"You don't have to tell me."

"I know. Maybe that's why I can. My aunt and uncle made it very clear to me that I couldn't turn into my mother, that if I did, they would disown me as they had her."

Sam frowned. "What did she do that was so terrible?"

"She ran away with my father."

"She ran away with a man she loved? And I assume he loved her."

"I think so. I was so young. My aunt always said that my mother had brought terrible disgrace on the family name. My mother never married him, you see."

He rose then and pulled her into his arms. Illegitimacy. No, that wasn't something that would sit well with the Potters. He tamped down his anger. "I'd say she was a pretty gutsy lady. And you're lucky to have inherited some of those guts, A.J."

When she simply laid her head against his chest and tightened her hold on him, the sweetness of the gesture streamed through him. He was beginning to understand the reasons for the tough A.J., and the soft and sweet Arianna. And he had more questions, but for now, all he wanted was to hold her.

"I shouldn't be doing this," A.J. said as she drew back. "I don't want you to get the wrong idea. And you've made it clear that you have trouble with rules. But if we're going to be partners until we find Pierre, I'd like our relationship to be business."

"We're going to be lovers, Arianna." Taking her hand, he raised it to his lips. "We can postpone it for a while, but it is going to happen. What I can go along with is that we can wait until we figure out who snatched Pierre and why."

WE'RE GOING TO BE LOVERS.

The words spun through A.J.'s mind as she watched Sam clear the plates from the table. She knew it was true. It wasn't just when he kissed her. All he had to do was look at her in that quiet intent way he had, and an image filled her mind of exactly what it might be like to make love with Sam Romano. To have his hands on her. She couldn't seem to take her eyes off his hands as he measured coffee into a filtered cone and filled the pot with water. Not a movement was wasted. Sam Romano was a man who would be competent at any task he put his mind to.

He hadn't touched her yet. Not really. But every time she thought of what it might feel like, her throat went dry.

She had to stop thinking about it. She had to keep her mind on business. Pierre Rabaut had been kidnapped that afternoon—right in front of her eyes.

Sam pulled two mugs from the cupboard, then glanced at her. "Would you like some? I always think better when I'm mainlining caffeine."

A.J. held out a hand for the mug. "Me too. I was just thinking..." Ruthlessly she focused her mind on what she should be thinking about. "Why would anyone want to kidnap Pierre?"

He leaned against the counter. "It all goes back to the necklace. I know that you don't want to believe that he stole it, but two people besides me were waiting for him outside the museum that morning. One pulled a knife on him and the other tried to run him down. I'm not the only person who thinks he took the necklace. I did some research this afternoon. I told you before that Pierre used to be a master jewel thief, a real legend. I researched him when I was a kid and sort of made a secret file on him. He started when he was in his teens and his MO was to hit only museums. Until today I thought he'd never been arrested."

"But he was?"

"Once. I did some research after I dropped you at your office this morning. I wanted to find out all I could about the Abelard necklace, and Pierre's name popped up. He stole the Abelard necklace forty years ago. Or at least he attempted to steal it, and he got caught. And it wasn't a museum he hit, but a private home. More like a castle really. It belonged to an old, respected family, the LaBrecques, just outside of Rheims. From what I could access, Pierre was caught with the Abelard necklace on him, thrown in jail, and he was all set to go to trial when the charges were suddenly dropped."

"Why?" A.J. asked.

"I couldn't find details, just a brief statement that Pierre had been released. A month later, he was in New York." Pausing, Sam sipped his coffee. "When I was very young, Pierre used to entertain me with stories of this clever jewel thief. But he was a good thief. He always put the jewels back at the end of the stories. I would never have put the stories together with Pierre if I hadn't heard him and my father talking one night. I was eleven at the time, insatiably curious and ready to idolize a jewel thief. It sounded romantic. When I asked Pierre about it, he told me that he had erased that part of himself, that life, when he came here, and he wouldn't talk about it. Now, he was just a jazz club owner, nothing else. Gradually, I began to idolize him for that."

A.J. studied him for a minute, picturing in her mind the curious little boy. "So you found out what you could from other sources."

Sam grinned, his eyes filling with laughter as he reached for her hand. "What can I say? Forbidden fruit. I've never been able to resist it. Besides, I had a knack for research, even back then. I love the New York City Public Library, the smell of the books."

"I know," she said. "Every time I came home from boarding school, it was my refuge."

For a moment their eyes met and held, and A.J. felt the warmth steal through her right down to her toes.

"We might have been at the library together and never known it," Sam mused. "I don't suppose that you ever made love to anyone in the stacks?"

"Of course not." But the image of making love with Sam there slipped so easily into her mind.

He raised her fingers to his lips. "We'll definitely have to try it some day."

Drawing in a deep breath, A.J. pushed the image out of her mind and withdrew her hand from Sam's. "We have to concentrate on finding Pierre. Why that particular necklace?

Why then and why again now? Mind you, I'm not agreeing that he stole it this time, but I'm willing to concede that you saw him go into the museum and come out."

"At least I'm making progress."

"Why don't we call Rheims? Maybe someone at the police station would remember the case and fill in some of the blanks."

He shot her a speculative look. "Do you speak French?"

"Yes. I spent a semester studying in Paris."

"You'll have to have a cover story—a student doing research on the necklace, the legend behind it. Where's your phone?"

Turning, she led the way into the living room. "There's a legend behind the necklace?"

"Yeah. I read up on it this afternoon. Throughout the ages, the owners have all lost their true loves—or some bunch of nonsense like that."

A.J. glanced down at her skirt. Of course, it was nonsense. She didn't believe that a skirt could help you find your true love any more than a necklace could make you lose him.

"Damn."

She glanced up to see Sam hanging up the phone.

"What?"

"I forgot about the time difference." He glanced at his watch. "It's only about 3:00 a.m. in France. We'll have to wait till tomorrow."

Once again, A.J. caught a glimpse of the frustration and the fear that Sam was so careful to keep on a tight leash. She went to him. "There must be something we can do tonight." For a moment the words hung in the air between them. It had grown dark in the apartment. Behind Sam, framed in the window, the lights of Manhattan had winked on. For a moment, neither of them said a thing. All that could be heard was the steady hum of the air-conditioning unit in the window.

"Sleep," he said. "It's been a very long day. The police are working on tracking down who rented the van and the limousine. Andrew will call if there's news. And we'll both be thinking more clearly in the morning."

It wasn't disappointment she was feeling. Sleep was the sensible thing for both of them. And A. J. Potter was always very sensible.

"Sam, I—" A.J. wasn't sure what she might have said, what she might have done if she hadn't been interrupted by the ringing of a phone. Not the one he'd just hung up, but her cell phone. She felt almost as though she were pulling free of a magnetic tractor beam as she turned and walked to the table where she'd left her purse. Her phone was ringing for the fourth time when she lifted it to her ear. "Hello?"

"We have Pierre." The voice was low and tinny sounding. A.J. felt a sharp arrow of fear spear through her. "We will exchange him for the necklace."

"Where have you got him?" She felt Sam cover her hand on the phone and tilt it so he could hear too. "Is he all right?"

"If you want to see him again, you'll have to do exactly what you are told. Tomorrow you will be given instructions about when and where to deliver the necklace."

"But I don't—"

"Tomorrow."

"Did you hear me? I don't have the necklace. Where is Pierre?"

There was no answer.

"They cut the connection," Sam said.

"They've got Pierre, and they think I have the necklace. What are we going to do?"

Sam's eyes suddenly narrowed on hers. "Maybe you do have the necklace. It would explain a lot."

"Explain what?" A.J. asked, then stared as Sam grabbed her purse from where she'd dropped it on the table and up-ended it. The contents cascaded out onto the table—a note-book, sunglasses, a wallet, a leather-bound checkbook and her Palm Pilot. She saw a glint of metal, a flash of a clear blue stone just before something else landed at her feet with a clatter.

Even in the dim light, she recognized the sparkle of gem-stones and the gleam of gold.

6

"I STILL CAN'T FIGURE OUT how it got into my purse."

Stuffing his cell phone into his pocket, Sam glanced at the necklace that was now lying spread out in a circle on the glass-topped coffee table. Multicolored gems were caught in whisper-thin twists and loops of gold. Unable to help himself, he picked it up to examine it more closely and sank onto the sofa next to A.J. The necklace was lighter than he would have thought. The pure artistry of the craftsmanship had fascinated him from the first moment he'd seen it in the case at the museum. It was a piece that might tempt the most reformed thief out of retirement.

"The how is easy," Sam said as he set the necklace back on the table. "Pierre used to do all sorts of sleight of hand tricks to amuse me when I visited his club as a child. I think he may have been a pickpocket before he went after bigger prizes. The when is trickier." He'd given it some thought while he poured them both more wine. And he'd been turning it over in his mind while he called the detective handling the kidnapping and updating him on the ransom call. Then he'd left a message with his brother Andrew's paging service. "I'm betting Pierre slipped the necklace into your purse after that pickup truck nearly ran both of you down."

A.J shook her head. "No. When I first raised my head and saw his face, I thought he might be dead. He was definitely out cold for a few minutes."

"What about during those few minutes when neither one

of us was paying any attention to him?" Sam could still recall exactly what had happened when he'd held her hand and looked into her eyes. Time had ceased to exist and his whole world had narrowed to her.

Suddenly, he frowned. "Hell, that was the second time you made me lose track of everything. The first time was when you came striding down the street toward me in that skirt. I felt as if I'd been struck by lightning. I never even saw that bearded guy pull the knife."

Shifting his gaze, he focused his whole attention on the skirt. She was sitting in the corner of the couch, her legs tucked under her, and the skirt had once more inched its way intriguingly up her thighs. It was clearly going to be the death of him.

Reaching out, he captured the edge of the hem and rubbed it between his fingers. The texture was soft and silky smooth, a hint of what her skin might feel like. He was tempted to lower his hand, just a whisper, and test his assumption when something in the dark fabric caught hold of the light and shimmered. Sam felt a tingling heat, not unlike a low-level electrical current, shoot up his arm.

"There's definitely something about this skirt. I told you I had some experience with it before," he added, keeping his voice even. The tingling sensation was gone, but he couldn't release his hold on the thin, silky material.

"You did?"

He thought it was a frown he heard in her voice. But he couldn't seem to take his eyes off the skirt either. Fascinating. "Not up close and personal, like this. I was hired to keep an eye on this woman who was wearing it for some articles she was writing. She was calling it the *man-magnet skirt.* I got to witness firsthand its effect on her boss and a troop of Cub Scouts at Rockefeller Center. It was total mayhem, and it might have saved her from being hurt. I never got close enough to touch it though. And now I can't seem to let go of it."

"That's ridiculous," A.J. said. When she took hold of his hand, the skirt slipped from his fingers. "See?"

He met her eyes then. The tingling sensation flowing up his arm was much stronger, hotter than when he'd been holding the skirt. "Thanks. I much prefer holding on to you."

Her eyes narrowed. "You're a very sneaky man, Sam Romano."

"You bet."

When she tried to pull her hand away, he tightened his grip.

"Sam—"

Whatever else she would have said was forestalled by the ringing of his cell phone. He was still grinning when he released her hand to reach for it. But it was relief he was feeling. He was a man of his word. Always had been. But if they hadn't been interrupted, he wasn't at all sure he would have honored the word he'd given to A.J. His gaze shifted to the skirt. It packed a punch all right. And as fascinating as that was, he was all but sure that the woman wearing it packed an even bigger one. And she was slowly but surely eating away at his control.

"Yeah?" he said into the phone.

"What the hell are you doing having me paged?"

The moment he heard Andrew's angry, disgruntled voice, he burst into a laugh. "Why did I have them page you in the middle of the night, bro? Simple. I wanted to say I told you so in person. I told you that the necklace in the museum was a fake, and tomorrow I intend to prove it to you. I just want the name of that medieval-jewelry expert you used on the LaFevre case last year."

A.J. STUDIED SAM as he filled in his brother on the call from the kidnappers. But he wasn't going to mention the necklace they'd found in her purse. He'd told her that he wanted to keep his options open, that they might need it to get Pierre back.

His explanation made sense. So why was she so sure he wasn't telling her everything?

Because Sam Romano was...complicated. A mystery. He had as many facets as the carefully cut stones in the Abelard necklace. There was that innate kindness. And understanding. No wonder he was so easy to talk to. She'd never told anyone, not even Claire and Samantha, the things she'd told Sam tonight. And he hadn't judged her. He'd merely accepted her. Each time she looked at him, each time she went up against him head to head, she found something different. Something new.

And she wanted him. She still hadn't recovered from what she'd seen in his eyes a few minutes ago before the phone call had interrupted them. There'd been a recklessness in them that she'd found almost irresistible. For one breathless moment she'd been sure he was going to kiss her again. She wanted him to kiss her, and it wouldn't have stopped there. Though he'd held only her hand, she'd had a vivid impression of what it would be like to lie beneath him on the couch. She'd imagined so clearly the softness of the cushions against her back, the hardness of his body pressing against hers. Her stomach turned a fast, hard somersault just thinking about it.

"Did you guys in blue get a name to go with the license plate on the green van or the limo yet?" Leaning back, Sam grinned. "Sure, I've got Luis at the office running the number. But you guys got a head start. Yeah?" Reaching into his pocket, Sam pulled out a notebook. "Patrician Limousine Service and Vans Are Us. Yeah, I got it. Let me know what you find out when you check the rental records. In the meantime, I'm going to sweet-talk the jewelry expert you mentioned into doing a little off-the-record work."

It wasn't too late, A.J. thought. When he was finished with the phone call, she could take his hand and draw him to her. He wouldn't resist, but she didn't think he'd make the first move. No, he would want to keep his word. The decision would have to be hers, and she wasn't sure she had the courage or the confidence to make it.

A.J. pressed a hand against her stomach as it took another hard tumble.

Sam suddenly muttered something in Italian. To A.J., it sounded like a curse. Then after a brief pause, he threw back his head and laughed. "Of course, I'm in shape for the game on Sunday. The McGerriety family doesn't bother me."

The sound of Sam's laughter filling the room was so infectious that A.J. wanted to join him. It would be fun to be able to call up a brother or a sister and tease them, laugh with them. In all the years she'd spent in her uncle and aunt's house, she couldn't recall sharing a laugh with any of them. Family dinners had been downright funereal. Her Uncle Jamison had been reserved and stoic. Her aunt had run the meals as if they were a board meeting, with each person required to report on his or her day in detail. And, of course, there was a quiz. Then there was Rodney—snide, sneaky and just a little on the stupid side.

Glancing around the apartment, she bit back a sigh. There'd been lots of shared laughter with Samantha and Claire, but in a few weeks their lease would be up.

"Where were we?" Sam asked as he pocketed his cell phone. "Ah, yes. We were talking about your skirt. A more cynical man than I might think you wore it this morning purposely to distract me."

She stiffened. "You think I wore this skirt to—? Now wait just a minute." Swinging her legs to the floor, she stood up.

"Are you insinuating that I was somehow involved in this jewel heist? Maybe I should review a few facts for you. Number one," she held up a finger, "you still don't have any proof that the Abelard necklace has even been stolen. The one in my purse could be a fake. Number two, I never met your godfather until this morning." She grabbed his chin and lifted it so that his eyes met hers. "I think you should stop staring at my skirt and pay attention."

"I think it would help...if you pulled it down." His voice sounded strangled. "Just a little."

A.J. glanced down at the skirt. It had hiked its way almost up to her— Releasing her grip on Sam's chin, she grabbed two handfuls of the hem and gave it a swift, hard tug. The skirt slithered smoothly to her knees. "There," she said, dancing back and forth on her feet to make sure it was going to behave. "It's got this tendency to hike up."

"I NOTICED," Sam said. Boy, had he noticed. And the fact that she'd pulled it down wasn't helping a damn bit—not with the light behind turning it transparent. He shifted his gaze to the necklace and waited for the blood to return to his head. "Not that I'm complaining." He raised one hand, palm out to her. But he kept his eyes on the jewels. "And just for the record, I was not insinuating that you might have had anything to do with stealing the Abelard necklace."

"I still don't believe that Pierre stole the necklace."

"I admire your loyalty to your client. But the evidence is sitting right on the table in front of us. Pierre had a copy made of the Abelard necklace—one good enough to fool the museum curator and the insurance people, at least temporarily. He made a switch, placing the fake necklace in the display case and carrying this one out of the museum. When he realized that he was about to get caught, he put the real necklace in your purse. What other explanation is there?"

"This one's the fake."

"Wishful thinking, counselor."

She put out her hand. "Care to wager an Alexander Hamilton?"

"Ten bucks? That's pretty low stakes."

He glanced at her hand, then met her eyes. "I've got a better idea. If the necklace in the museum display case is a fake, I get to plan a date for just you and me that will last an entire weekend."

A.J.'s eyes narrowed. "Did anyone ever tell you that you have a one-track mind?"

Sam grinned at her. "All the time. You're not afraid to agree to the wager, are you?"

A.J.'s chin lifted. "No. If you win, you get a weekend date. But if this necklace is a fake, then I get a weekend's worth of free investigative hours. I could use someone like you on some of my pro bono cases."

Sam took her hand. "Deal. Andrew gave me the name of a medieval-artifacts expert who works right at the Metropolitan Museum. First thing in the morning, I'm going to set up an appointment. Once this expert identifies the one in the display case as a fake, I'll make arrangements at that place I told you about for our date. Make sure you're free next weekend."

She pulled her hand away. "You're awfully sure of yourself."

"Yeah, I am." Picking up his wineglass from the table, he took a long swallow. "Pierre took the necklace. It's the only theory that fits what happened today. I thought at first he passed it to the bearded man. And he might have intended to until the guy pulled a knife on him. Could have been a double cross, and that's why he put it in your purse. And that's why that same bearded friend tried to snatch your purse in front of the precinct this morning. He must have figured Pierre had to pass it off to you."

"So you figure they were after *me* in front of the courthouse."

"And Pierre. That way they'd be sure to get their hands on the necklace."

"You're building a very strong case," A.J. said. "And it's all based on the fact that you've lost your faith in your godfather."

"Yeah." Sam picked up his wine and drained the glass.

"Why? Why are you so willing to believe that he would give up the new life he's built for himself just to steal that necklace?"

"Because people disappoint you. Sometimes they can't help it." He thought of the photo she still kept on her bedside table, and of the story she'd told him earlier. And he thought of his own father and the affair he'd had for almost twenty years with Isabelle Sheridan. "There are times when you want things to be different, but it just doesn't work out that way."

Her hands closed over his. "You really don't want to be right about Pierre stealing the necklace, do you?"

Sam laced his fingers with hers as he turned his gaze back to the necklace. "I was hoping all along that I was wrong. But if Pierre didn't steal the necklace, why are they holding him for ransom?"

"You think they'd believe him if he told them, 'Hey, I didn't steal it after all?'"

Sam studied her for a moment. "You've got a point, counselor. But if this necklace on the table is a fake, why did Pierre plant it on you? Why didn't he just tell me what was going on and that the authentic Abelard necklace was in the museum?"

A.J. rolled her eyes. "Oh, I don't know. Let me take a big

leap here and guess that there may have been some male pride involved. Maybe he'd rather you'd believe that he could still pull off a big heist."

For a moment, Sam said nothing. He just studied her. She was making sense. Maybe he was taking too narrow a view of the case. More than anything he wanted to pull her into his arms and just hold her. But he already knew with little doubt that if he touched her now, he wouldn't be able to stop. And he could still see that she wasn't ready yet. He could see the nerves in her eyes, all but feel them in the tension that had already started to build between them. And she was exhausted. Why hadn't he noticed that before?

"Dammit."

She looked at him curiously. "What?"

"Just when I've got this fantasy going of making love to you for seventy-two hours straight, you've got me worrying that I might lose my bet." He had the satisfaction of watching her eyes cloud and feel her hands tremble before he carefully released them.

He had to be crazy, he thought. Probably certifiable. They were alone in her apartment, there was a bedroom right down the hall, and he didn't have a doubt in the world that he could overcome any objections she might have.

But he'd given her a promise.

"I'll figure out something." Definitely, he promised himself. "But not tonight. Tonight, we're going to get a good night's sleep."

When the apprehension shot to her eyes, he continued. "We have a lot of work to do in the morning. So, you're going to sleep in your bedroom, and I'll take a nap here on the couch until your roommates get back."

As he watched her rise and walk down the short hallway, Sam told himself that he would laugh at this someday, maybe when he was Pierre's age. The thought of his godfather had him glancing back at the necklace and frowning. They would get Pierre back, he told himself.

But knowledge was power. Fake or authentic, the answer to what was happening to Pierre was in that necklace. He was sure of it.

A.J. WOKE the way she always did—all at once. But she didn't open her eyes. Instead she lay perfectly still, hoping as she did so that she might be able to fall back into the dream she'd just tumbled out of. It had been about…Sam.

With a slight frown, she searched her memory for the details. Images flashed through her mind—running down a dark alley after a man holding the Abelard necklace over his head like a banner. Every time he'd been caught in a splash of light, she could see the man she was chasing was Sam. And the need to catch him had been so sharp, so compelling.

If she was going to spend the night dreaming about him, why couldn't her subconscious mind have conjured up that seventy-two-hour date he'd described?

Is that what she wanted?

The question, along with the strong scent of coffee, had her opening her eyes and sitting straight up in bed.

"It's about time," Samantha said, settling herself on the foot of the bed and handing A.J. a mug.

"We didn't want to wake you," Claire said as she unseated the red fox and dropped herself in the rocking chair.

"But we didn't want to leave without talking to you," Samantha explained.

"Yes, tell us everything," Claire said. "It's not every night we come home and find a cute detective sleeping on the living room couch."

A.J. took a swift gulp of her coffee and tried to gather her thoughts as Cleo hopped up on the bed and settled herself on the pillow. A.J. scratched her behind the ears. "What are you doing here?"

"Mrs. H. has an appointment at the beauty salon and then she's got an appointment at the kennel," Samantha explained. "That's the other reason we have to talk to you. It didn't work well to bring Cleo with her to the kennel yesterday. She—Cleo, not Mrs. H.—still goes into attack mode when she sees one of those pedigreed studs. The owner of the St. Bernard threatened to sue. The owner of the dalmation nearly attacked Mrs. H."

"She wants us to baby-sit Cleo for the day," Claire explained. "And I have to help Petra set up her gallery for the show. There'll be instant bedlam if I take her there with all those nude men walking around."

"And I have an event at the hotel," Samantha said. "Can you handle it?"

"Sure," A. J. said. "I don't have to go to the office because it's golf outing day, and she gets along well with Sam."

"Sam would be the cute detective?" Samantha asked.

"His real name is Salvatore but he prefers Sam," A.J. said.

Samantha's smile spread slowly. "I like him already."

"I'm sorry. He must have frightened you when you came in and saw him on the couch," A.J. said.

"No, not at all," Claire said. "He'd asked Franco to warn us, and he gave us his card and showed us his license."

"He also told us that someone tried to kidnap you," Samantha said. "Are you all right?"

A.J. took another long swallow of her coffee as she tried to gather her thoughts. She didn't want to worry either Claire or Samantha. "It's a long story, and I don't even know all of it yet. But Sam and I are going to find out."

Claire and Samantha exchanged glances.

"Is he the one?" Claire asked.

"The one what?" A.J. asked.

"The one—you know—the one the skirt worked its magic on?" Samantha prompted.

"No," A.J. said with a quick shake of her head. "He's the homeless man though—the one I thought the skirt might work its magic on, but of course it turns out that he isn't homeless. He was working undercover trying to catch a jewel thief." Pausing, she drew in a deep breath and took another sip of her coffee. "It's very complicated, but I'll try to give you the short version."

When she finished, Samantha was pacing back and forth in the space between the foot of the bed and the dresser and Claire was just staring at her, a worried expression on her face.

"I'll be all right," she assured them both. "The police are working on finding Pierre. And Sam and I have agreed to work together until we straighten out this whole mess."

"He does look like a man who can handle himself in a dark alley," Claire said.

"He can," A.J. said. "And his brother is a policeman—a detective."

"Except for the kidnapping part, it would make a great date story," Claire said. "Would you mind if I use it in my research?"

"Sam and I haven't had a date," A.J. said quickly. "You know I've sworn off dating."

Samantha held up four fingers and ticked them off one at a time. "He brought you home, fixed you dinner and he kissed you twice. You've got to admit those are four elements of a fairly typical date."

"And you like him, don't you?" asked Claire.

A.J. met Claire's eyes first and then Samantha's. Finally, she sighed. "Yes. I do like him, but—"

"Oh, I know all about *buts,*" Samantha said with a laugh.

"*But* why does he have to come walking into my life right now? *But* why does he have to be so attractive?"

"*But* he's not what I expected. *But* I'm not ready for this," Claire added.

"We made a deal," A.J. said. "We're not going to date. We're just going to work together."

"Cool," Samantha said. "That's one way to really get to know a person."

"She knows some things about him already," Claire pointed out. "He was gentleman enough to sleep on the couch to protect her until we got home. And she knows how he kisses."

"He can make my mind go blank," A.J. said.

"Let's drink to that," Samantha said. They tapped their mugs together and drank.

"Even putting Mr. Sam Romano's kisses aside, in one day, you got yourself a client and your uncle assigned you to a court case—which you handled successfully. Plus you managed *not* to get yourself kidnapped. I'd say, all in all, the skirt did quite a job for you."

A.J. turned with Samantha and Claire to study the object in question, which was visible in the open door of her closet.

"It looks so ordinary," A.J. said. She furrowed her brow. "Except that it seems to ride up my legs when I walk. And Sam says it feels like silk."

"Interesting," Claire said. "Someone mentioned to me that it's transparent. But I can't see it."

Samantha walked to it and rubbed the hem between her fingers. "Men like to touch it. They can even smell something, but I can't smell a thing."

Claire tilted her head to one side. "Ordinary looking or not, it certainly seems to have a siren's pull on men."

"Are you going to be wearing it again today, A.J.?" Samantha asked.

A.J. hesitated for a minute. But the moment she realized that she was thinking of wearing it to attract Sam Romano, she said, "No."

"Then I'll hang it back in my closet," Samantha said. "And I'm going to be needing it this afternoon—there's a huge event at the hotel. I'll need all the help I can get. Will that be all right with the two of you?"

"I was planning on using it tonight. It's Petra's art show, and I thought I'd wear it for the bachelor auction," Claire said.

"Go ahead," A.J. said. And then the thought suddenly struck her. She'd promised her uncle that she would go to her aunt's cocktail party. "No, wait. I almost forgot that I have to go to one of my aunt's parties. This time I get to meet a prospective client instead of the usual prospective husband, and I could really use that skirt. Would it be available between, say, four-thirty and seven-thirty?"

"Sure," Samantha said. "We'll just have to work out a time-share. I can have it back here at four-thirty."

"I don't need it until seven," Claire said.

"Then I'll be back by then," A.J. said.

"Sounds like a plan to me. Now, I have to go." Samantha grabbed the skirt. Halfway to the door, she pulled a note out of her pocket and turned back. "I almost forgot. Your Sam left this for you."

A.J. waited until her roommates were gone before she opened the folded sheet of paper.

"I'll be waiting for you in the lobby at 9:00 a.m. sharp. Wear casual clothes and shoes appropriate for running—just in case. Sam."

Just in case she had to chase him down an alley for real?

A.J. read the note again. It was brief, businesslike—the kind of note a man might write to his partner. With a sigh, she glanced down at Cleo.

The dog sighed too.

"At least you know what you want and you go for it," A.J. pointed out. "I wish it were that simple for me."

"Mrrrrrmph," Cleo replied.

"Sam seems so sure of what he wants." Just thinking of his words, of the intent way he always looked at her, had an arrow of heat shooting through her. A.J. scratched the poodle's head. "I can just imagine what your Dr. Fielding would say about my dream."

"Mrrrrrmph," Cleo repeated.

Lifting the note, A.J. read it again. There wasn't any indication in it at all that there was anything between Sam and her but a job. Fine.

She glanced at her watch. 8:00 a.m. First she'd make the call to Hancock, Potter and King and remind her uncle's secretary that she was taking the day off. Then she would have almost an hour before she met Sam, and it was early afternoon in Rheims. Pushing Cleo gently aside, she leapt out of the bed.

PACING BACK AND FORTH in the lobby, Sam glanced at his watch for the third time. It was 9:03. Except for yesterday, A.J. was never late.

"I'll buzz her in just a moment, and let her know you're here," Franco offered from his spot in the pool of sunshine pouring through the skylight. Wearing tights that were cut off at the knees and a matching lime-green tank top, the doorman was practicing what looked like yoga exercises. Franco was seated with his legs folded one over the other and his arms extended, palms upward into the sunlight. "I don't like to interrupt my morning routine. Yoga helps me maintain the flexibility that is so essential in the martial arts."

"You're sure she's still up there?" Sam asked.

Franco gripped one of his ankles with both hands and

raised it slowly over his head, then settled it across his shoulders. "Positive. No one gets past this desk without my seeing them."

Sam believed him. No one entered or left the building without Franco buzzing them through the door and grilling them on some aspect of their lives.

A.J. was safe. And he was being ridiculous. When he'd left at around 2:00 a.m., there'd been a giant, dark-skinned man on duty at the desk, and Tyrone had been in place across the street. The giant had identified himself as Franco's cousin and he'd assured Sam that no stranger was ever allowed into the building on his shift.

But that hadn't prevented the worry from eating at him and threading its way into what little sleep he'd managed to grab. That one fact more than anything had convinced him that he needed her with him today. Oh, he'd debated about leaving her behind, making her promise to stay in the apartment.

It might even have been fun to have that particular argument with her just to see the way her eyes lit up when she got angry. But he knew that keeping her within arm's reach was the only way he was going to be able to focus on getting to the bottom of what was going on with Pierre. Besides, that razor-sharp mind of hers was going to come in handy.

Lifting his hands, he flexed them and shook them out. His feeling that something bad was going to happen had increased steadily in the hours since he'd left A.J.'s apartment. It told him that a clock was ticking.

"Before you go up, you think you might give me a hand with this?" croaked Franco.

Sam was startled to find himself in front of the elevator door, punching the button.

Turning around, he saw that Franco had managed to turn

himself into a human pretzel. He hurried toward him. "What can I do?"

"Grab...my...left...foot."

Sam hesitated. "The one on top?"

"Yeah," Franco managed. "Now...push down...on my head and—"

The leg suddenly sprang free and slammed into Sam's shin.

"Sorry," Franco said on a grunt as he began to massage his calf. "Cramp."

"That kind of thing happen often?" Sam asked, resisting the urge to follow suit and massage his shin.

"Only when the weather is going to change. I should have checked with the weather channel before I tried it." Reaching up, Franco unwrapped his other leg from around his neck, placed it on the floor and sprang to his feet. "Look sharp. Your date's here."

"I'm late."

Sam turned to watch A.J. stride across the lobby with Cleo in tow. She was wearing snug-fitting black pants that ended midcalf, a white T-shirt and black low-heeled sandals. But it wasn't the clothes that riveted his attention and made his throat go dry. It was simply A.J.

"I hate to be late. But I was on the phone with the police station in Rheims." She waved a sheaf of papers at him. "I told them I was a freelance writer doing research on the Abelard necklace and that I was hoping to sell the piece to *Metropolitan* magazine. They faxed me the police report of the original theft. Wait till you see! There's a woman involved."

There was a woman involved, all right. Sam couldn't take his eyes off her. Her eyes were lit with excitement, triumph. Energy all but poured out of her, enough to send Cleo skittering around in circles on the marble floor. The realization shot through him that he'd never wanted her more. So much for all of the careful resolutions he'd made during the night to be patient and give her time.

He wasn't sure in that moment that either one of them could control the timetable of what was going to happen between them. Grabbing her, he swung her around in a circle. If they weren't standing in the middle of a hotel lobby with glass doors facing the street—and a doorman who would have been perfectly happy to act as voyeur—Sam was sure he would have made love to her on the spot.

"And Mr. Romano and I are not dating," A.J. said to Franco as soon as she was on her feet again. "We are merely working on a case together."

"I see," Franco said. "What kind of a case is it?"

Seeing the gleam of curiosity leap into Franco's eyes, Sam said, "We can't talk about it. Client confidentiality. And we'll be officially dating next weekend. I have to win this little bet first." Then grabbing A.J.'s hand, he pulled her toward the door.

Franco paused with his hand above the buzzer. "And when the case is solved, I'll get all the juicy details?"

"Scout's honor," Sam promised. But he waited until they were out on the street before he breathed a sigh of relief.

"Sorry," A.J. said. "I said too much in there. I was just so excited. I never did anything like that before. I just told a whopper of a lie over the phone, and the man at the other end believed me. He faxed the official stuff from the file, but he also told me the gossip."

Sam grinned at her. "Welcome to the fun side of a P.I.'s life. I'm about to introduce you to the more dangerous side."

"What's that?" she asked as he raised a hand and had a taxi careening to the curb.

"We're going to search Pierre's office."

7

"SO YOU THINK Pierre had a ladylove and that's why he stole the Abelard necklace forty years ago?" Sam asked as he paid off the taxi and joined A.J. and Cleo on the curb.

"Tried to steal it," A.J. said. "He was caught and arrested with the necklace on him."

"Right," Sam said. The official police report had contained only the bare facts. The necklace belonged to Girard LaBrecque, a rich vineyard owner, and Pierre had been found at the foot of one of the battlements of his castle with the necklace on his person. One week later, LaBrecque dropped all charges and Pierre was released.

"But you believe the theft had to do with a woman."

"That's what the man I talked to believes. Girard LaBrecque and Pierre Rabaut were both in love with the same woman, Marie Bernard. Marie was engaged to LaBrecque, and he had promised her the necklace on their wedding day. Then she met Pierre and broke off her engagement. It caused quite a scandal. Her parents didn't approve of Pierre. He was a nobody, a stranger in town, and Girard came from their social sphere, and the marriage had been arranged for some time. Pierre left town as soon as he was released from jail, and Marie married LaBrecque. I'm betting she did it to save her true love from jail."

"I'll bet she did it because she decided that she couldn't marry beneath herself."

A.J. studied him for a minute. "I didn't peg you for a cynic."

"I didn't peg you for a romantic." And he was absolutely sure that she didn't think of herself that way. "Plus, your theory doesn't explain the big *why*. Why did Pierre steal the necklace in the first place? My guess is that his *true love* wanted to marry him and still get the necklace. So he tried to steal it for her."

"You think she wanted to have her cake and eat it too?"

"You got it." Taking her arm, Sam steered her past two stores just opening for business. In front of the third one, he paused to inspect a basket of apples. "Some women are like that."

"Are you speaking from your own experience or from your father's?"

"Both, I suppose," he said as he busied himself selecting a perfect apple. "But I may have given you the wrong impression about my father and Isabelle Sheridan. They were both very happy with the arrangement they had."

"But you weren't."

Sam looked at her, surprised to see both interest and understanding in her eyes. "He said I would understand someday." Reaching out, he tucked a strand of hair behind her ear and gave in to the urge to let his fingers linger there.

He was almost getting used to the constant, humming desire to touch her. To kiss her. He'd lost sleep last night thinking about doing just that. And more.

"I think you're wrong about Marie Bernard."

He watched her chew on her bottom lip, oblivious to the thoughts racing through his mind.

"If what you're describing had been the case, if Marie Bernard had wanted him to steal the necklace for her and then decided to go with the rich guy when he failed, why did he fly over to France for her funeral three months ago?" she asked.

"Where did you learn that?"

"The policeman I talked to was very chatty. He said that Pierre's visit was all anybody talked about for weeks afterward. It stirred up the whole scandal again. Mr. LaBrecque and his son were *not* pleased."

Sam thought for a minute, tossing an apple into the air and catching it. "And the Abelard necklace goes on tour three months later. This is getting curiouser and curiouser."

"Exactly. No thanks," A.J. said when he offered her an apple.

"Take it," Sam said in a low tone. "Pretend you're inspecting it. I need a moment to see if we were followed."

She did exactly what he asked without missing a beat. He glanced in the window, but the street seemed empty. Looking past A.J., he saw that no cars had pulled to the curb since they'd alighted from the taxi, and no pedestrians had stopped anywhere near to browse. And she was still looking at the apple, turning it over in her hand as if it held the secrets of the universe. She'd make a damn good operative.

"See anybody?" she asked.

"No. Want me to buy that for you?"

"Thanks, but no," she said as she returned it to the basket.

Taking one more quick look around, Sam linked her hand with his and steered her past the next store and into the alley.

"I thought we were going to Pierre's apartment," she said.

"The first time I kissed you was in an alley, and now that I know you're a romantic—" her quick unladylike snort had him grinning "—here we are."

She glanced around. "Pierre doesn't live in an alley."

"No, he lives above his club. We're going in the back way."

"And we're not going in the front way because...?"

"Number one, I don't have a key, and number two, if there's anyone in the club, I don't want them to know we're here."

"You know, it has not escaped my attention that you are mocking me when you do that number thing. I don't recall that Sherlock ever mocked Watson."

"Me?" He pressed his hand against his chest. "Mock you? Never. Haven't you ever heard that imitation is the sincerest form of flattery?"

"Right. Let's table that for now, and you can explain to me where the back entrance is."

He pointed to the fire escape.

Not batting an eye, she met his straight on. "You get to carry Cleo."

"No argument? No complaints? I may have to marry you," he said conversationally as he reached up to pull the ladder down. And where in the hell had that come from? he wondered as he pulled himself up to the first rung. Sam Romano never used the M word. He never even thought it. On the second rung, he turned to glance back down at A.J. She was staring at him, her mouth slightly open, her expression as shocked as he felt. There was some satisfaction in that.

"Penny for your thoughts, counselor."

He watched her gather herself, narrow her eyes. "A romantic and a cynic? That sounds like a match made in hell."

She was quick all right. "Maybe," he said as he bent down and held out a hand, "we can both give it some thought. Right now, give me Cleo."

She did without a word.

Cleo whined and wiggled.

"It's all right, girl." He tightened his grip on her as he climbed to the first landing. The moment he made it, A.J. grabbed on to the bottom rung and swung herself up behind him.

"What are we looking for in Pierre's apartment?"

"I wish I knew." He patted the dog's head and settled her more firmly against him as he began the climb to the next landing. "Anything that might shed some light on what's happening."

Cleo wiggled in an attempt to get out of his arms.

"Easy, girl. Are you afraid of heights?" Tightening his grip on her, he stroked her head.

"Bite your tongue," A.J. said as she joined him on the landing. "Dr. Fielding would love to hear she has some other sort of phobia."

"Aside from the one where she attacks her pedigreed lovers?"

"Would-be lovers. None of them was able to do the deed. According to Dr. Fielding, Cleo is seeking her true love. But let's get back to Pierre." A.J. began to pace on the fire-escape landing. "Marie dies, Pierre goes to the funeral, and the past is stirred up. What if the whole exhibition was set up to entrap Pierre?"

Sam turned it over in his mind. "Why?"

"Revenge for what happened in the past."

"But LaBrecque kept the necklace and got the girl."

"But Pierre went free. What if LaBrecque was never happy with that? Some men are very possessive."

Patting Cleo, Sam considered it. "And the hit-and-run is a backup plan to make sure that Pierre doesn't get off this time?"

"Exactly."

"And the kidnapping is because Pierre got the necklace and got away with it."

A.J. shot him a look. "I'm not going to stipulate that. How about LaBrecque *believes* that Pierre got away with the necklace?"

Sam let the possibilities swirl around in his mind.

"Men have been known to do strange things for love," A.J. said.

"But in this case, the woman's dead and LaBrecque had her for forty years."

"Okay. Now's the time for you to come up with a better idea, Sherlock."

Sam grinned at her. "Sure thing. I think we have to look for more pieces to the puzzle. First up, we need to dig up more on the LaBrecques, and second, we need to check Pierre's apartment."

Cleo sighed on his shoulder.

"She seems much quieter now," A.J. said with a grin. "It's time to make our move."

Neither of them spoke as they climbed up to the last floor. Sam handed her the dog, then tried the window and found it locked. Taking a thin wire out of his back pocket, he slipped it between the upper and lower sash.

"You didn't mention we were going to break in," A.J. said.

"I did mention I was going to show you the dangerous side of the P.I. business." The lock snicked open. Withdrawing the wire, he pushed the window up. "And that I don't have a key."

"And if we get caught?"

"You'll say your client gave you a key, and that we're just looking for clues. That will be half true." He grinned at her as he threw one leg over the sill. "Or you could wait here."

"No," she said as she wiggled through the window with Cleo in tow and joined him in the narrow hallway.

Sam finessed the wire into the lock on Pierre's apartment door.

"You've done this before," A.J. said.

"Not since I worked for my cousin, Nick. He closed down his agency two years ago when he got his law degree, and he urged me to work for Sterling Security. My assignments there are usually more high-tech—tracking down data, following the money trail."

Sam fumbled with the wire and nearly dropped it. Why was he telling her all this? he asked himself. He'd never been one to reveal much about himself. So why now? Because...well, she was easy to talk to, for one thing. The sharp mind and the challenging questions held a strong appeal.

But it was more than that. For a moment, he stopped fiddling with the wire to look at her. She was pacing back and forth in the narrow hallway with that no-nonsense stride of hers. And she was carrying a poodle in her arms, humming to it as she patted its head.

She might be all wrong for him—a rich princess to his pauper. But somehow she fit. He wanted her in his life.

"Earth to Romano."

"Hmmm?" he asked, realizing that she'd said something.

"If you're bored at Sterling, why do you work there?"

"Money. I can make a lot more there than I could on my own, and my family needs it. The hotel is in need of renovations. Plus, I wanted to learn the high-tech side of the business. That's where the big money is. But this part's more fun," he added as he finally heard the lock click.

When he pushed the door open, the idea of fun vanished. He heard her quick intake of breath, but that was the only sound she made. He already knew she had grit, but the violence of what he was looking at had his own stomach muscles tightening.

Books that had lined the shelves on three walls lay strewn across the floor. Lamps and chairs were overturned. A potted tree lay on its side with dirt sprayed in a circle around it.

"What were they after?" A.J. asked.

"I'd say the necklace. They're pretty sure you have it, but they had to make sure."

Cleo growled deep in her throat, then gave a yip. Sam

reached for his gun with one hand and shoved A.J. behind him with the other.

When the barking started, it took him a minute to realize that it wasn't coming from Cleo. Motioning A.J. to stay where she was, he threaded a path through the debris. Some years ago, Pierre had adopted a dog he'd found in the alley, or the dog had adopted him. Antoine was a thoroughbred mutt with street smarts, Pierre had claimed, something that papers and a pedigree couldn't provide.

Edging his way into the hallway, he saw that all four doors were shut. A loud crash to his right immediately narrowed his choices. It was Pierre's bedroom, if he recalled correctly. "Antoine?"

There was another crash.

"Antoine, sit."

There was a louder crash and the door trembled.

"Antoine, sit," Sam repeated, praying that the dog would remember his voice. It had been a while. After counting to ten, he opened the door two inches, then let out the breath he'd been holding. Antoine was sitting on the other side, looking very large and thumping his tail on the floor.

"You remember me, don't you, boy?" he asked as he held out his hand.

As Antoine began to sniff his fingers, Sam glanced around the room. This one was untouched. Evidently, the intruders had decided not to mess with Antoine.

"Good boy." He was patting the dog's head when Cleo suddenly pulled A.J. into the room.

For a moment, the two dogs merely stared at one another.

"Cleo, be good," A.J. said. "What is...that?"

"Pierre's dog. I'd forgotten all about him, or I would have come sooner. He can't stay here."

"What breed is he?"

A very cagey one, Sam thought. Antoine had remained

seated and was allowing Cleo to come closer for a sniff, letting her get used to him. "Not one that Mrs. Higgenbotham would be looking for, if that's what you're thinking."

"It's what they're thinking," A.J. pointed out.

Cleo had progressed from staring and sniffing to nuzzling.

Sam grinned. "What can I say? Old Antoine works fast."

"Not any faster than my girl," A.J. said with a grunt as she yanked on Cleo's leash. "You keep your eye on him. I'll handle...her."

She led the way back into the living room, dragging a reluctant Cleo by her collar. Antoine rose slowly to his feet, and Sam could have sworn the dog swaggered as he followed the two females. "I know exactly what you're thinking," he said to the dog. "Good luck."

"Bite your tongue," A.J. said.

A.J. KNEW what the dogs were thinking too. The moment she'd gotten back to Pierre's living room, she'd settled herself in a chair and pulled Cleo to the floor at her feet. Antoine had made himself comfortable on the back of an overturned leather chair directly across from them. He looked perfectly relaxed, except for his eyes. They were fixed on Cleo, willing her—no, challenging her—to come to him.

It reminded her of the look she'd seen in Sam's eyes more than once—the look of a man who knew what he wanted and also knew that it was only a matter of time before he got it. A tremor moved through her at the same time one moved through Cleo.

"He's dangerous, girl," A.J. said in a low voice.

"Cleo probably finds that very attractive," Sam said. "If your theory is correct, that's probably why Marie Bernard was attracted to Pierre. He was the tough, street-smart thief. She was a well-brought-up and wealthy young lady."

A.J. glanced at him. He was bent over Pierre's desk, his

brow furrowed in concentration, as he pulled out a drawer and began to run his hand over it inch by inch.

"Mrs. Higgenbotham will have a fit. She's bound and determined to mate Cleo with another pedigreed poodle."

Sam shifted his glance from one dog to the other before he turned the drawer upside down. "Didn't the dog shrink say that Cleo was searching for her true love? Maybe she's found him."

"Forget it, Cleo." She patted the poodle's head while she kept her eyes on Antoine. "This one is not for you."

Antoine kept his eyes steady on Cleo.

If it were any other dog, she might have labeled him an over-confident jerk. But A.J. had to admit Antoine had a certain...charm. Not unlike Sam. The dog was tough-looking with a strong, sleek body covered with short hair that wasn't quite gray, but not quite brown. The eyes were the same unnameable color, and his face looked as if he had a permanent grin on it. She could certainly understand Antoine's attraction. He was darn near irresistible.

Her gaze shifted to Sam. He reached to snap on the desk lamp and held the back of the drawer close to it. Light shifted across the planes and angles of his face as he frowned in concentration. There was a hint of danger about him too. She'd seen it even when she'd thought him homeless.

The chant started again. *This is him. This is him.*

And he was just as impossible for her as Antoine was for Cleo.

Cleo let out a soft sigh, filled with longing. Or was it her own sigh that she heard? For her true love?

No. A.J. dismissed the idea along with the chant. The whole idea of finding your true love was ridiculous. Was she actually going to let an overpriced dog shrink and the legend of a skirt influence her thinking this way?

What she was feeling for Sam was desire, plain and simple. She shut her eyes and then opened them again, and watched him press his fingers slowly and surely along the inside edge of the drawer. He'd begun to whistle between his teeth—a happy tune that had her smiling and wondering if it was a habit he'd developed in his childhood. She wanted to know more about his childhood. She wanted to know more about him.

She wanted *him*. She couldn't look at him without feeling her pulse speed up. Nor could she block the memory of what his taste had been like—dark and dangerous, just as he was. He still hadn't touched her, not really. But she thought she knew how it would feel to have his fingers skimming over her in that same slow, careful way they were moving over the inside of the drawer. And she could have his hands on her now if she wanted. All she had to do was go to him and…

When he glanced up and his eyes met hers, she rose to her feet and took two steps toward him.

"I think I've found it."

"Hmmmm?" She tried to rein in her thoughts, tried to focus.

"There's a false bottom in this drawer and there's a spot to push that releases a spring. Pierre showed it to me once when I was a kid. I thought I forgot where it was, but I think he's glued it shut." Pulling a penknife out of his pocket, he began to work it along the side. "Could you come here and hold the drawer?"

It took all of her strength, all of her determination, to do what he asked. Even then, when she gripped the edges of the drawer and his fingers brushed against hers, she felt her bones melt.

Wood splintered.

She tightened her grip on the drawer and concentrated hard. "Why didn't they find this?"

Sam flashed her a grin. "Look at how much trouble I had,

and I knew where to look. Besides, they were sloppy. I figure they came in after the club closed, let's say around 3:00 a.m. That's when Pierre's manager leaves. They had four, maybe five hours. If they hadn't been amateurs, they wouldn't have left all this mess."

He skinned his knuckles and shook his hand. "Damn. Here, let's set it on the desk."

He dug the penknife in again, and pried the false bottom open, inch by inch.

Beneath it lay a paper folded neatly. Sam opened it and spread it out on the desk.

Sam. Things are not always what they appear to be.

"Any guesses on this one, Sherlock?" A.J. asked after a moment.

Sam sighed. "Only the obvious—that he left it for me. He'd know that if anything happened to him, I would look here."

"Well, I think it means that he didn't steal the necklace."

A sudden noise from the hallway had them both turning toward the door. She just had time to note that it was ajar before Sam stuffed the paper into his pocket and pulled them both down behind the desk. A second later, his gun was out.

The sound came again—someone brushing against the wall?

Their faces were close, and Sam barely breathed the words. "Stay here and be quiet."

A.J. waited, her heart in her throat, as he rose and soundlessly made his way to the door. She was going to count to ten before she followed. One…two…three…four…

There was another noise. Listening hard, she tried to place it. Above the brushing noise, she heard a…moan? The sound of the door closing had her jumping to her feet. Sam was standing there, grinning from ear to ear. "Cleo finally got her man."

"No." A.J. made it across the room in three strides. "I've got to stop them."

Sam took her by the shoulders. "I really wouldn't advise it. Antoine's not such a nice guy when he gets ticked off."

"But—"

"If you interrupt him now, he's going to be very ticked off. Take it from me. It's a guy thing."

"But they can't." But when she tried to pull away, he merely tightened his grip on her.

"They already are. The least we can do is offer them a little privacy."

Giving up, A.J. rested her head against his chest. She could hear his laugh bubble up, and she couldn't prevent a smile. "This is not funny. What am I going to tell Mrs. H.?"

"True love conquers all?"

She looked at him then, expecting to see laughter in his eyes. But it was something else that she saw—something reckless and wicked. And there was a ruthless impatience too. This wasn't the laid-back, charming man she'd grown to know. This was someone who would reach out and take what he wanted.

And she would love it.

Then just as she was ready to throw caution to the wind, Sam sighed and laid his forehead against hers. "I gave you my word, Arianna. But this whole partnership thing would be a heck of a lot easier if you were as ugly as Watson."

A.J. wasn't sure whether she wanted to laugh or cry when he threw a friendly arm around her and drew her toward the door.

SAM'S OFFICE WAS a far cry from the P.I. offices she'd seen depicted in movies. It had none of the usual Sam Spade decor.

First of all, it was neat as a pin. On one wall, floor-to-ceiling windows offered the familiar view of Broadway and Times Square that was frequently seen on TV or in print.

Sam hadn't said more than two words to her since they'd walked in. Turning, she studied him, sitting behind his glass-and-chrome desk, playing two computer keyboards with all the concentration of a concert pianist at his Carnegie Hall debut. He was expecting a call back from a medieval-artifact expert at the Metropolitan Museum at 10:30 sharp. But if he got a refusal there, he intended to have a backup expert he could call on.

The high-tech work might not be as exciting as the work he'd done for his cousin, but he looked to be very good at it.

When the phone rang, Sam reached for it and then began to charm the expert on the other end of the line. Glancing at her watch, she decided to time him. Then she let her gaze wander to Cleo and Antoine, who were cuddling in the corner, looking very satisfied.

Everything had been so simple for them. They saw what they wanted and took it. She wanted Sam. He wanted her. Maybe she ought to stop overanalyzing the whole thing and just follow Cleo's example.

Her gaze shifted to Sam, and the expression on his face, the look in his eye, was more than enough to tell her that the medieval-art expert was a woman.

"Sure, I can be there in fifteen minutes, Doc. See you then." The moment he hung up the phone, he glanced at the two sleeping dogs. "We can't take the dogs. Plus it's a shame to wake up the star-crossed lovers. If we left them here, they could at least spend the day together before they have to be separated forever."

"No. I'd better take Cleo home and face the music. And I have a hunch you'll do better with your art expert if I don't tag along." Rising, she walked over to pick up the leash.

Antoine shot to his feet and growled. An instant later, Cleo was at his side, growling too.

"Time for a backup plan," Sam said. "I suggest taking them both with you. Let them plead their case to your Mrs. H. If worst comes to worst, she can turn the problem over to the dog shrink. Even as a layman, I can spot a case of separation anxiety. I'll send Luis with you." Pausing, he glanced at his watch. "I should be at your apartment in a couple of hours. Stay put until I get there."

"And if the kidnappers call?" They hadn't talked about the fact that they hadn't received a call yet.

"You still stay put until I get there," Sam said. "And they will call. Making us wait is part of their strategy. They want us as worried as possible."

"I've got to go to my aunt's cocktail party tonight from five to seven. I gave my uncle my word."

"You didn't mention that before."

"No." Nerves had formed a hard knot in her stomach. "I...I don't look forward to them, but I...." Dammit, if Cleo could do it, so could she. "I'd like you to go with me."

"Arianna." He learned back in his chair and smiled at her. "Are you asking me out on a date?"

She straightened her shoulders. "You could call it that."

"I'll do that." There was pleasure in his eyes, and that had her courage increasing.

"Five o'clock sharp," A.J. said as she moved toward him. "My aunt doesn't like to be kept waiting." Reaching into her purse, she pulled the necklace out and placed it on his desk. "You're going to need this. And this."

Grabbing the lapels of his jacket, she pulled him into a kiss. Surprise. She saw it in his eyes, and had a moment to glory in it before his lips turned hot and hard on hers. She'd meant to control both the kiss and her reaction to it. Both intentions faded the moment that the fresh wave of desire moved through her. Each time it did, the need became hotter, more potent. Irresistible. When she drew back, she wasn't sure who had proven what to whom.

THE ROOM WAS DIM, except for the high-intensity beam of light that held the necklace prisoner on the table. The woman, Dr. Candace Lowe, was bending over the table, fingering the intricately woven metal that held the jewels in place. She was in her fifties, a small round woman with intelligent blue eyes, who'd already informed him once that her examination couldn't be rushed.

Sam stamped down on the urge he had to pace. It would only distract her. And she was taking long enough as it was.

She hadn't spoken for...Sam glanced at his watch. A minute. Had it only been a minute since she'd told him that the gems were real?

Dammit. He had to get control. A.J. was fine. Luis would see to that.

And he should be thinking about the necklace. If the one on the table was real, then Pierre had stolen it from the museum, and the one in the display case was a copy. That would mean he'd been right all along, and he'd won his wager with A.J. He should be thinking of the long weekend they could spend together in the penthouse apartment on the roof of his family's hotel.

Taking his eyes off Dr. Lowe, he switched his attention to the dust motes swirling in the thin beams of sunlight shooting through the high barred windows. It was only helping a little to think about spending the weekend with A.J.

Dammit. He hadn't wanted to be right about his godfather. In spite of what he'd seen, he didn't want Pierre to have stolen the necklace.

"The necklace is a fake," Dr. Lowe said.

Sam jerked his attention back to the table and the jewels

glowing in the high-intensity beam. "I thought you said the gems are real."

Dr. Lowe smiled at him. "They always are in the best fakes. And someone went to a great deal of trouble and paid a pretty high price for this one. The way the gems are cut date from the time period. It's the metal that isn't authentic. The patina is wrong."

"You're sure?" Sam asked. He should be feeling relief. But his fingers had begun to tingle.

She met his eyes. "Positive. If you need more convincing evidence, there are tests that could be run. But they will only confirm what I've said."

"There's another necklace—perhaps the real one—on display at the Grenelle Museum a few blocks from here. Would you be willing to take a look at it?"

Her brow shot up. "*Perhaps* the real one? Do you think there might be two fakes?"

Sam winced a little. "It doesn't sound so good when you put it that way, but I'd just like to be sure."

Dr. Lowe glanced at her watch. "What the heck. A nice little walk in the sunshine with a handsome man? It's the best offer I've had all day."

With a laugh, Sam held out his arm for her. "I like your style, Doc."

A.J. PAID THE TAXI DRIVER and unloaded the dogs onto the sidewalk. Then, for just a minute, she hesitated. It was the first time since she'd signed the lease with Samantha and Claire that she'd dreaded coming home. But it was always better to get unpleasant tasks over with quickly.

"C'mon, guys," she said as she strode forward.

Cleo whined a little as though she knew what they were going to face once they were inside the Willoughby.

Sun glared off the glass doors and prevented her from seeing into the lobby until she'd pushed her way through them. Her heart sank when she saw a uniformed cop in deep conversation with Mrs. H.

Her first impulse was to run. Where?

Antoine and Cleo both began to bark at the cop. When he whirled around, it took A.J. a moment to recognize Franco.

"Oh, hush up, you...oh, my." He paused for a moment to stare at Antoine. "You are a big one. Keep a firm grip on that leash, A.J. I need this uniform intact tomorrow. I have a walk-on part on a soap."

"Got it," A.J. said. "He's a friend, Antoine."

To her surprise, Antoine sat down at her feet, and Cleo sat beside him.

"What breed is he?" Mrs. Higgenbotham said, wafting toward them.

A.J. considered for a moment. It would be easy to lie and to postpone the consequences for a while. Until their lease was up, perhaps? But it would only compound the injury when Mrs. H. found out the truth.

"Mixed. As I understand it, his owner, who is a prominent business owner in town, found him in an alley. But he's been raised in a good home. He has his shots." At least she hoped Antoine did. She figured Pierre was a man who would take care of anyone he cared for.

Mrs. H. glanced dubiously at Antoine, then her eyes widened as Cleo snuggled closer to him.

"She likes him," Mrs. H. said.

A.J. drew in a deep breath. "She likes him a lot."

The dogs had progressed from rubbing against one another to nuzzling.

"I guess so. This is going to get X-rated in another minute," Franco said, an unholy glee filling his eyes.

Mrs. H. shot him a look, then fixed her gaze on the dogs.

A.J. cleared her throat. "It's already gotten X-rated once,

Mrs. Higgenbotham. I guess you could say it was love at first sight, and I tried to keep my eye on Cleo, but—"

"Are you saying they've already...mated?" Mrs. Higgenbotham asked.

"Yes."

"And they're about to again. I don't think I can allow that in the lobby," Franco warned.

"They can't," Mrs. Higgenbotham said, grabbing Cleo's leash. "Just who is this prominent businessman?"

"Pierre Rabaut. He owns a jazz club."

"I'm going to sue him," Mrs. H. said, pulling Cleo's leash. "You can handle it for me, Ms. Potter. I want compensation for the pain and suffering, plus what I would have gotten for Cleo's first litter if she had mated with one of the dogs I had lined up at the kennel. Come...on...Cleo."

But Cleo was not coming willingly. She was hunkered down on her belly, and Mrs. H. was dragging her toward the elevator. Antoine, also on his belly, was moving alongside her like a commando.

Franco was doubled over, holding his sides. A.J. sincerely hoped he would wrinkle his precious uniform.

"Look, Mrs. Higgenbotham, I'd be happy to handle your case." That was a lie. She couldn't sue one of her own clients. "But before you do that, I think that you should check with Dr. Fielding."

"You do?"

"Definitely." Ignoring Franco's muffled laughter, she hurried on. "Didn't Dr. Fielding say when he regressed her that she was just looking for her true love? What if he's right?" A.J. prayed that lightning wouldn't strike her. "What if Cleo has found her true love?"

Mrs. H. had stopped pulling on the leash, the dogs were rolling around together and Franco had completely disappeared behind his desk. She could hear him pounding on the floor.

"You think...?" Mrs. H. was staring at Antoine.

"Romeo and Juliet, Hamlet and Ophelia, Antony and Cleopatra," A.J. said.

"You could be right," Mrs. H. said. "All I've ever wanted was for my Cleo to be happy."

"Yes," A.J. said. A quick glance at the dogs told A.J. that Cleo was close to becoming very happy indeed.

"There's only one way to settle this. I'm taking them both to Dr. Fielding," Mrs. H. said, grabbing the leashes and pulling both dogs toward the door. "Franco?"

There was a muffled sound from behind the desk.

"Pick yourself up from the floor and call Dr. Fielding's office. Tell them I'm on my way."

A.J. stared in astonishment as the seemingly helpless Mrs. H. sailed out the door with the two dogs in tow. They seemed perfectly happy to go with her now that she wasn't set on separating them. "What's gotten into her?" A.J. asked as Franco finally reappeared above his desk.

"Nothing at all," he said, wiping tears of laughter from his eyes as he picked up the phone and punched in numbers. "That's the real Mrs. H. She only digs out the billowing caftans and dyes her hair pink during the summer when she wants to take advantage of Tavish Mclain's renters. The other nine months of the year, you'd swear she's the reincarnation of General Patton."

"THE MUSEUM WILL BE CLOSING in fifteen minutes." The guard who'd entered the room through the archway addressed the remark to the air above their heads. Dr. Lowe had hunkered down in front of the glass case so that she could view the necklace at eye level. Before that, she'd spent a good bit of time viewing it from above, using a jeweler's eyeglass.

Sam said nothing, but if she needed a few extra minutes, he was fully prepared to distract the guard.

"I'd like to get my hands on it and feel the weight," she said. "Just to test the difference between this one and the other."

"Then this one is real?" Sam asked.

"That depends on what you mean by real," said Dr. Lowe, meeting his eyes. "From what I can see this necklace is a perfect match to the other one, right down to the patina on the metal."

Sam's eyes narrowed. "Then...you're saying..."

"That this is not a necklace that dates back to the twelfth century. I can't be sure without running further tests when it was made, but I'd be willing to make a fairly goodsize wager that it was made by the same person who created the other one."

"Then where in the world is the real Abelard necklace?" asked Sam.

Dr. Lowe's brows shot up. "You're the detective, Mr. Romano. You tell me."

8

TURNING, A.J. studied first one profile and then the other in the mirror. It had been a long time since she'd given any thought to dressing with the sole purpose of pleasing a man. She'd teamed the little black skirt she'd bought at Bloomingdale's with a matching halter-backed top and high, strappy sandals. All in all, the result was anything but conservative. Her shoulders, back and legs were bare. Of course, she could always wear a jacket. She turned again. Maybe she'd just take it with her and carry it over her arm.

Sam had checked in with her twice since she'd come back to the Willoughby. The second time was to tell her that he'd won their little wager. The necklace in the display case at the Grenelle Museum was a copy. But the one from her purse had been a copy too.

In spite of the fact that he'd told her just how and when he intended to collect on his wager, she could tell that he was worried about Pierre. And so was she. Knowledge was power. But so far nothing they'd learned was helping them find Pierre. Turning, she walked to her purse and opened her cell phone. She'd checked it three times since she'd come home to make sure that it was working and that she hadn't missed a call. So far, the kidnappers had not contacted her with any more information.

Turning back to the mirror, she gave the outfit a final once-over. Tonight she wanted to make Sam Romano think only of her. After the business of her aunt's cocktail party was over, she had a plan. She was going to seduce Sam Romano.

She glanced quickly at her watch. Samantha was late with the skirt, and A.J. needed it for the cocktail party. There was that prospective client that her uncle had described—the one who wanted to be represented by all of the Potters. This could be a chance for advancement at the firm.

A.J. stopped short and stared at herself in the mirror. She hadn't given two thoughts to her uncle or the law firm or the new client all day. Slowly, she sank down on the bed. Sam Romano was really getting to her.

And who was she kidding? She wanted to wear the skirt because of Sam. Just the thought had nerves knotting in her stomach. So what if she'd never really set out to seduce a man before? If Cleo could, she certainly could.

The moment she heard Samantha enter the apartment, A.J. stripped out of her skirt and raced from the bedroom. "Thank heavens you're back. I really need that skirt, and I have to get to Aunt Margery's by 5:00 sharp."

"Sorry. They kept asking questions." Samantha slipped out of her skirt and took A.J.'s. "I've got to run back there. The Family Values Folks think I'm checking in at the office. Oh, and by the way, the cute detective with my favorite name arrived at the same time I did. I left him pacing back and forth with Franco in the lobby."

A.J. zipped the skirt and then turned in a full circle. "What do you think?"

"I think that the cute detective is in deep trouble."

"I hope so." A.J. took two steps toward the door, then stopped and turned back. "I really hope so. I...you're sure you don't need the skirt?"

Samantha took her hands. "I'm positive. Go for it."

Drawing in a deep breath, A.J. nodded, then glanced at her

watch. "At seven I'm handing off the skirt to Claire. I feel like I'm in a relay."

"I'm just happy that my lap is over."

"Wish me luck," A.J. said as she hurried out the door.

"WELL, WELL, WELL. You certainly do clean up nicely, don't you?" Franco said to Sam.

Sam paused in his pacing. He had to because Franco had stepped smack into his path.

"Nice threads," Franco said, a note of envy in his voice. "You look as comfortable in that tux as you did in those rags you wore the other day. Very suave, very James Bondish."

"Thanks, I think," Sam said, taking note for the first time of Franco's costume of the day. "You make a pretty convincing cop."

Franco's chest puffed out. "Thanks. I landed a part on *Desires.* I tape on Monday, and I'm trying to get the feel of the character. Jack Nicholson says the clothes do it for him—get him into the role, I mean."

Sam glanced down at his tuxedo. Maybe the tux would do it for him—get him into the role he wanted to play tonight. He had a plan and it was complicated by...everything. It wasn't just the multiple copies of the Abelard necklace or Pierre's disappearance. The biggest complication was going to step out of that elevator at any minute. He was nervous. He hadn't had this many butterflies flapping around in his stomach since he was...in his teens maybe. Glancing down, he saw that he was in danger of crushing the small bouquet of flowers he was holding. Violets. He'd stopped on impulse to buy them because they made him think of her.

"Excellent choice in flowers, by the way," Franco said. "Her colors are light spring, you know. Perfect."

Perfect. That was just the word Sam would have used to describe A.J. as the doors of the elevator slid open and she strode toward him. The combination of white skin and black silk was dazzling. He would have said so if the breath hadn't simply left his lungs. He did open his mouth, but not a sound came out.

It helped a little that as soon as she saw him, the familiar focused look disappeared from her face and she stopped dead in her tracks to stare at him as if she'd never seen him before.

"Excellent! Oh, this couldn't be better. Twice in one day! True love in the lobby of the Willoughby."

Franco's staccato babblings and the fact that he was jumping up and down and clapping finally shook Sam loose from his trancelike state, and Sam summoned up the strength to offer A.J. the violets. "Hello. You certainly don't look like a lawyer."

She smelled the flowers, then smiled at him. "You don't look like a homeless person."

He grinned at her and held out his arm. "Touché. Shall we go?"

As she slipped her arm into his, Franco raced to the door and held it open. "Have fun, you two."

A.J. STOPPED SHORT the moment they were on the sidewalk in front of the Willoughby. A long, silver-colored limousine was parked in front of the curb and a uniformed man smiled at her and opened the door.

"What...?" she began. But Sam was already taking her arm and urging her forward. "You didn't have to...." But she was happy that he had as she slid onto the leather seat.

"I wanted this evening to be special," Sam explained as he took a champagne bottle out of ice and dealt with the cork. "It's our first real date, and I wanted to surprise you. How am I doing?"

"Fine," she said. "Great." *He* surprised her. He looked

perfectly at home, as if he spent every day riding around in limousines. And she could barely get out one-word sentences. This would never do.

"I figured that you were used to this kind of thing." He handed her a glass.

She glanced around the limousine and then back to him. It suddenly occurred to her that he was showing her that he could fit into her world. The sweetness of the gesture streamed through her, and she felt her heart take a tumble.

"To our first date," he said as he touched his glass to hers.

She'd had a plan for the evening—to seduce Sam Romano. But she'd intended to wait until they'd gotten through her aunt's cocktail party.

"To our first date." She took a sip of her champagne and let the bubbles tickle her throat. Later, there might be a message from the kidnappers. Later, she would have to hand the skirt off to Claire. Right now...she thought of how Cleo might handle the situation.

"You're very quiet," Sam said. "Is something wrong?"

"I was just thinking..." A.J. glanced quickly around. The partition between the driver and the passenger area was closed so that they had complete privacy, and there was an intercom for communicating with the driver. Yes, it just might work. Then she met Sam's eyes. "Since I asked you out, don't you think I should be the one to surprise you?"

"Sure," he said.

"I thought that I was going to take you someplace special after the cocktail party. But I have an even better idea." Handing him her glass, she prayed that her hand wouldn't shake as she pressed the intercom button.

"Yes?"

"Would you please drive through Central Park and take the long way to that address we gave you?"

"Certainly."

"And we don't want to be disturbed." Her heart was beating so hard she thought it just might pop out of her chest when she turned back to Sam.

"A.J., I—"

"I have two things to say. Number one, I want to make love to you, and number two, I want to do it right now."

There was surprise in his eyes, but there was delight too. And that had any remaining doubts streaming away. With a slow smile, she hiked up her skirt and straddled his lap. Then framing his face with her hands, she leaned down and brushed her lips over his.

Sam gripped her shoulders with his hands. "A.J., we shouldn't."

She nipped sharply on his bottom lip before she drew back. "Now a simple *no* might have stopped me. But a *shouldn't?* Not a chance."

She heard the low sound of their laughter blending in the air as she leaned in to kiss him again. Nothing had ever felt so good, so right. And in a blink, whatever advantage she'd had by surprising him had vanished. His mouth was hot and hard on hers.

He demanded. She gave.

She hadn't thought it possible to feel so much—the press of his hands on the back of her head, the scratch of his teeth on her neck. The heat that sprang up between them offered a sharp contrast to the cool swish of air from the air-conditioner vent.

When he allowed her to pull back, she said, "I want your hands on me. You've made me wait so long."

With his eyes on hers, he traced his fingers down the length of her neck, then slipped them beneath her halter until they cupped her breasts. A thousand pinpricks of pleasure danced along her skin.

Slowly, she trailed her fingers down his neck, then flattened her hands on his chest. His heart pounded against her palms. There was such strength there and such kindness too. And she knew that it was more than desire that was pulling her. It was the man, himself. Leaning closer, she began to nibble on his lips. "We'll have to be very quiet. And quick."

When she pulled the clasp of his belt free and slipped down his zipper, she heard his quick intake of breath. Even as the thrill of power moved through her, she wanted more. He'd moved his hands from her breasts to push up her skirt. Then his fingers began to toy with the lace banding her thigh-high stockings. This time the pleasure that spiked through her was so sharp she was sure she was going to shatter.

"I planned on taking this slowly the first time," he murmured against her mouth. His fingers began to trace a lazy pattern on her thighs, higher and higher.

Trailing a line of kisses along his jaw, she closed her teeth on his ear at the same moment that she slipped her fingers beneath his waistband. "Think again."

He arched upward. "Touch me."

She closed her hand around him at the same moment that he slipped a finger into her. Pleasure and power streaked through her.

Then at long last, he did move quickly, positioning her legs. He was even quicker with the condom, ripping open the foil and sliding it on. She helped him, pulling aside the thin lace of her panty. And then she watched him push slowly into her.

Dizzy with the pleasure of it, she met his eyes, and what she saw in them—the heat, the longing—was enough to start the first convulsion. As it streamed through her in an ever-widening wave of pleasure, she tightened her arms and legs around him.

Sam watched the pleasure stream through her. It seemed

to him he'd waited forever to see A.J. like this. To be able to give her this.

He waited, keeping his own needs on a tight leash until she collapsed against him. Then, tightening his grip on her hips, he began to thrust into her, one stroke and then another. The third time he pushed into her, she began to move with him, settling into his rhythm. Each time he sank into her silky heat, he seemed to go deeper and deeper, losing more and more of himself. Then he felt the tension begin to build within her again, tighter and tighter.

"Now," she said.

The one word was enough to shatter the thin grip he had on his control.

And the one word was all it took to bring them both to a shattering release.

WHEN HE COULD THINK CLEARLY enough to move again, Sam lifted A.J. and set her carefully down beside him. Then he wrapped an arm around her and pulled her close. In another minute, he was sure he'd find the energy to speak.

"Well." A.J. stretched like a satisfied cat. "I have never seduced a man in a limousine before."

He tightened his grip on her. "I'm available anytime you want to give it another whirl."

When she lifted her head and he saw the reckless and amused glint in her eye, he laughed and kissed her nose, then gave her a hug. "You're incredible. And dangerous." And as amazing as it was, he wanted her again. Regretfully, he dragged his thoughts away from temptation. "I'll offer you a deal, counselor. The next time we make love, I want to be able to take my time—slow and easy—and savor every part of you. We'll do it right after your aunt and uncle's party."

"You drive a hard bargain," A.J. said. "The least you can do is offer me some more champagne before we get there."

"We're already there."

She stared out the tinted windows. "You're telling me that we're parked in front of my aunt and uncle's building? For how long?"

"The limo stopped moving a while ago. I was a little distracted at the time."

A.J. leaned over to straighten his tie, then used a napkin to wipe lipstick off his mouth. "How do I look? The doorman knows me. If he suspects...he'll tell my aunt's maid. After that, it might as well be on a billboard on Times Square."

Sam grabbed her hand. "You don't want your family to know about us?"

"You don't understand." She dropped to her knees on the floor to straighten the skirt. "How do I look?"

She looked frightened. And it was that alone that kept him from saying, *Make me understand, A.J.* There would be time later for that. Right now, he wanted to know exactly what kind of a family A.J. Potter had.

He raised the hand he still held in his to his lips. "You look lovely, except you might want to pull up those stockings. Have I mentioned that they drive me crazy?"

When he reached to help her adjust them, she batted his hands away. But her lips had curved, just a little.

He took her hands then and waited for her to meet his eyes. "It's only a party, A.J."

"Yeah. Tell me that when it's over."

AT THE DOOR of her family's apartment, A.J. hesitated. "I shouldn't have brought you."

"I'm not going to wait in the car, A.J."

"No. That's not what I'm saying." She reached for his

hand. "And it's not what I meant. Just promise me that you won't let them hurt you."

For a moment, Sam said nothing. Then he took her hand and raised it to his lips. "I'm a big boy. Why don't we just get this over with? Then I'm going to take you to that place I told you about. We won't be able to spend the weekend. But we can spend the night. And I will make love to you just the way I promised."

She nodded, then, still holding his hand, she opened the door and drew him with her into the foyer.

Aunt Margery swooped down on them immediately. A vision in deep amber, she managed to keep her smile in place when she shot A.J. a thinly veiled look of annoyance. "You're late."

"I'm afraid I'm to blame," Sam said with an easy smile. "I'm Sam Romano. And I apologize for crashing your party. A.J. and I had some business that ran late, and she invited me on the spur of the moment. I hope you don't mind."

"Business?" Margery asked.

"I'm with Sterling Security. You have a lovely home here."

"Thank you."

As she watched her aunt's look change from curiosity to dawning approval, A.J. let out the breath she hadn't been aware she was holding.

"There are several guests here who work in the financial district. Let me introduce you." Turning to A.J., she said, "Mingle. And pretend you're enjoying it."

A.J. watched her aunt lead Sam off with a mixture of relief and...loss. She had taken two steps after them, when her aunt turned around and pinned her with a look that commanded her to do what was expected of her.

"It's good to see you, Miss A.J. Might I say you're looking very fine tonight?"

She turned to smile at the butler who presented her with a glass of mineral water. "You always say that, Sweeney."

"It's always true, Miss. But it seems especially so tonight. Your uncle and cousin are closeted in the library with two of the guests. I'm supposed to let them know when you arrive."

"Do they want me to join them?"

"No, Miss. I'm just to let them know you're here. But there is another gentleman, a Mr. Chase, who asked for you."

Sweeney had no sooner said the name when A.J. spotted Parker Ellis Chase Senior moving toward her.

"Mr. Chase, this is a surprise. My uncle didn't mention that you would be here."

"When he invited me, I thought that I would be in Japan. But I rescheduled my meetings there."

"Does he know you're here? He's in the library."

"I came hoping that I could see you." He glanced at his watch. "But I have to leave. I'm having dinner with Park, and they eat early at Father Danielli's place."

"How's he doing?"

Parker Chase studied her for a moment. "Probably better than he would if he'd been released to my wife or me. And certainly better than if he had to go to jail. The hearing in front of Judge Stanton yesterday shook him up. Me too. I want to thank you for making arrangements at Father Danielli's. I was impressed with the little tour he gave me yesterday. I think Park was too. At any rate, at Father Danielli's suggestion, I struck a deal with my son. He stays there, and I'm going to try to get there twice a month and have dinner with him."

A.J. smiled at him. "Sounds like a good deal to me. Say hello to Park for me when you see him."

"I will," Parker Chase said as he moved past her toward the door.

A.J. began to make her way across a room crowded with

guests. Smiling, she joined in snatches of conversation here and there. By the time she made it to the French doors that opened onto the balcony, she'd garnered information on several of the day's golf scores, predictions on which way the numbers on the Dow would move on Monday and a review of the opening night of a new musical.

She could have listed each one of the topics in her sleep. Aunt Margery's parties were nothing if not predictable. When she spotted the tall blond man with the shoulders of a football player moving toward her, she took a quick look at her watch and smothered a yawn. It had taken less than five minutes for her aunt to sic bachelor number one on her. That set a new record.

"A.J.," the blond man with the very broad shoulders said. "I hope you don't mind. I'm Lance Foster. Your aunt promised me an introduction, but she seems to be busy."

She was very busy, A.J. noted, making sure that Sam was introduced to every eligible woman in the room. And he looked as if he were enjoying every minute of it. He was even flirting with her aunt. Her eyes narrowed as she studied him. He seemed to fit in here just as easily as he fit in with her roommates.

Other images slipped into her mind—Sam sitting on the sidewalk taking the money she put into his cup, Sam delivering a well-aimed kick to one of the bozos in front of the courthouse. The man had a knack for fitting in everywhere.

He'd even found a place for himself in her heart. Panic danced up her spine.

"I could give you a card."

"What?" A.J. reined her thoughts in and focused her attention on the man standing in front of her. For the life of her, she couldn't remember his name. And she didn't have any idea what he was talking about. "Your card?"

"My firm specializes in image consulting."

"Lance, give her a break. A.J. doesn't need an image specialist. She managed to steal a client right out from under my nose."

A.J. barely held back a sigh of relief when she turned to find Bob Carter at her side. She made no objection when he took her arm. Of all the men her Aunt Margery had set her up with Bob had been the least obnoxious. When they'd dated, he'd been fresh from a divorce, and once she'd made it clear she wasn't going to be part of his recovery process, they'd seen each other a few times just to talk shop.

"I've got to borrow her for a minute, Lance. We've got some business."

"I owe you one," A.J. murmured under her breath as Bob drew her away without waiting for Lance's reply. "In another minute I was going to yawn in his face."

"Well, maybe I should take you out on the terrace right now and you could show me your gratitude."

A.J. threw back her head and laughed.

"Thanks a lot. There are some women who would be eager to go out on the terrace with me."

"Too many women would. That was why we decided to stop dating and become friends."

"A fine friend you are. I shouldn't even be speaking to you after you took Pierre Rabaut's account away from me without even so much as a courtesy phone call."

A.J. turned to him. "I didn't even know he was yours. I got him out of some difficulty because I was on the scene, and I had no idea he was going to change law firms because of it."

"Relax," Bob said. "I'm not going to hassle you about it, especially now that I'm getting him back."

A.J.'s eyes narrowed. "What do you mean?"

Bob frowned. "You don't know?"

"What?"

Bob glanced around. "Look. I had his files all packed up

and ready to go this afternoon when I got a call from your cousin Rodney telling me that plans had changed. Hancock, Potter and King had just taken on a big client and there would be a conflict of interest. I shouldn't bother sending the files. Did I get it wrong?"

"Rodney got it wrong." A.J.'s mind raced. "Did he mention who the client was?"

"No."

A.J. thought of the two guests who were presently closeted with her uncle and Rodney in the library. "Do you have any idea what the conflict of interest might be? What's Pierre involved in?"

"Not much. He acquires real estate now and then. I handle those. And he consulted me a few months ago regarding something about an inheritance he'd come into. He thought there might be a problem collecting on it, and I referred him to Harry Simons in our estates department."

A.J. thought for a minute. "I'd like to talk to Harry as soon as possible. Can you arrange that?"

Bob sighed. "You expect an awful lot for a girl who won't go out on the terrace with me."

SAM FOCUSED half of his attention on the small talk that was going on around him, and the other half on A.J. She'd talked with three men so far, not that he was counting.

He wanted to blame it on the damn skirt. Then all he'd have to do was tell her she couldn't wear it again. But it was A.J. herself who was attracting men like honey drew flies.

Presently, she was deep in conversation with a slightly older man, good-looking. He'd made her laugh. No stars for that. Sam had had to stifle an urge to march over and punch him in his stomach. Right now, there was a frown on her forehead, and that meant she was interested in what he was saying. No stars for that either.

The real star was A.J. He couldn't seem to take his eyes off of her. He wanted to go to her right now, throw her over his shoulder and carry her off.

He forced his gaze to shift around the room, taking in the brocade drapes, marble floors, French doors leading to a sweep of terrace edged with a stone balustrade. The contrast between his sophisticated surroundings and his primitive urges had some of his tension easing.

So this was where she'd been raised. He'd pictured her in just these surroundings. But she didn't fit. And now that he was coming to know her, he understood why. The stir of anger he felt came from the recognition that she should have been made to feel as if she'd belonged here. And she hadn't.

"How did you meet A.J.?" Margery asked as she handed him a drink.

"My godfather recommended her," he said and sipped his drink. "Do you know that man over there talking to her?"

Margery glanced over toward the terrace doors. "That's Bob Carter. He works for Pitcairn and Cones, mostly as a hobby. His mother was a Penfield. They've always been heavily into real estate. I introduced him to A.J. and they dated for a while right after his divorce. I'm hoping to persuade her to give him another chance. They'd be perfect for each other. And it's time she married and forgot all this nonsense about being a partner at Hancock, Potter and King."

Sam didn't think they'd be so perfect for one another. Bob wasn't going to look so good with a couple of black eyes and a broken nose.

Margery put a hand on his arm. "If you're going to turn your business over to Hancock, Potter and King, you'd do much better to talk to my son Rodney. A.J. won't be with the firm long."

"Why not?"

"She's...flighty, like her mother was. But my son Rodney is steady as a rock. You can depend on him."

"Where is he?" Sam asked as he watched Mr. Perfect Match move away from A.J.

"Working," Margery said. "Why don't I just go and mention to him that you'd like to talk to him?"

Sam smiled at her. "I'd appreciate that."

A.J. had already begun to stride toward the terrace. He reached her just as they both stepped outside.

"YOUR FAMILY OUGHT TO BE lined up and shot," he said.

She stopped short and stared at him. His casual tone had her thinking she must have misheard him, but the hard, angry look in his eyes told her she hadn't.

"Have they always treated you like an unwelcome visitor?" he asked.

"Well..." It was exactly how they had treated her. She'd never questioned it, never blamed them for it, because they'd taken her in. "It's just that I've never been able to...fit in."

He took her chin and gave her a quick, hard kiss. "Thank heavens."

She'd just leaned into the kiss, begun to lose herself, when he withdrew. "What did Mr. Perfect Match say to you that made you angry?"

She had to struggle a minute to gather her thoughts and then suddenly her anger returned. "He told me that Pierre isn't my client anymore."

"He's heard from Pierre?" Sam asked as he drew her farther onto the terrace.

"No." Quickly, she told him what Bob Carter had said to her. By the time she was through, she'd begun to pace. Stopping herself, she turned to face Sam. "I'm not going to stop representing Pierre until he asks me to."

He smiled at her. "I know that."

And he did. She could see the understanding, the acceptance, in his eyes.

"You want some backup when you tell your uncle?" he asked.

She moved toward him then and took his hand in hers, felt how well it fit. "Sure. We're partners, aren't we?" There was more she wanted to say, needed to say, but first she had to talk to her uncle. Keeping a hold on Sam's hand, she led the way. The French doors leading to her uncle's library were about fifty yards ahead, blocked from view by a clump of potted trees.

When they reached the trees, A.J. heard voices. Peering through the greenery, she spotted Rodney, her uncle and two men in the library. One of the strangers was older, in his seventies or eighties, a tall striking man with white hair. He had a presence that radiated authority in spite of the cane he carried. The other man was tall also, and equally striking. She guessed him to be in his late thirties.

She'd started to circle the trees when Sam tightened his grip on her hand.

"...you understand I want Mademoiselle Potter to represent LaBrecque International."

"But, sir, I assure you that—"

Jamison Potter raised his hand to cut off his son. "Enough, Rodney. If Messiers LaBrecque want A.J., they will have her. But before I can agree to that I have to speak with her." He moved away from his desk, and drew Rodney with him toward the door. "Make yourselves at home, gentlemen. The view from the terrace is quite nice this time of year."

She and Sam had barely burrowed into the fake forest and hunkered down behind a large pot before the two Frenchmen walked out on the terrace. Seconds ticked by as the two men walked to the balustrade and finally came to a stop not ten feet away. A.J. was afraid to move, not that she could have. She and Sam were both on their knees and they were nestled as tightly together as spoons.

She tried to sort out the questions pouring through her mind. The older man had to be Girard LaBrecque, Pierre's old rival. He was the right age, though he hadn't kept as fit as Pierre. Why on earth did he want to hire her?

In just a minute she was going to unfasten herself from Sam and walk out there and ask him. But, at the moment, she was having trouble moving. How could she, when Sam was surrounding her?

She was even more aware of him than she'd been in the limousine. There, things had happened so fast. Wonderfully fast. Now, with his arms wrapped around her, all she could do was absorb the sensations. His chest was so hard where it pressed against every inch of her bare back. Her skirt had hiked up again, leaving her thighs bare too. She could feel the press of each one of his fingers where they rested right along the band of her stockings. The heat was so great, the need to move, to urge him to move, was so huge. She felt as if she were permanently trapped in a bubble of torturous pleasure.

It took every ounce of strength she had to focus on the two men when the younger one spoke.

"Papa...."

Girard LaBrecque cut him off with an impatient gesture. "I know what I am doing."

"Do you?"

The older man whirled on his son. "You dare to question me?"

"I mean no disrespect, and I held my peace in there. But we are alone now. And when Mother died, you promised me that I could finally run LaBrecque International."

"Yes. But you and I have decided to expand our distribution into this country. To do that, we will need legal representation here. This is a fine law firm."

The younger man began to pace. "I don't disagree with that. But this should be my decision. And you made the call without consulting me. Now I find it is not the law firm you want to hire. It is this A. J. Potter."

"I want her," the older man said, tapping his cane on the floor for emphasis. "When I saw her on TV yesterday, she reminded me of your mother."

"This is about that old rivalry, isn't it? She's Pierre Rabaut's attorney and so you want her. But we have bigger problems than that, Papa."

The older man tapped his cane again. "Nonsense! Rabaut took what is mine, and he still wants what's mine. He must be punished."

"It's LaBrecque International that we have to concentrate on. We should have expanded our markets years ago."

Behind the potted trees, A.J. turned to Sam, but he'd already read her mind. His hands had moved to her waist and he was rising, drawing her up with him.

"This is my chance." She mouthed the words to him, and he nodded in response.

A second later, she stepped out of the trees near the library doors and walked toward the two Frenchmen.

"I'm A. J. Potter," she said, holding out her hand the minute she reached them.

The older man grasped her fingers, then stared at her as he raised them to his lips. "Girard LaBrecque. And this is my son, Bernard."

A.J. would have extended her hand to the younger man, but Girard LaBrecque wasn't letting go of it. She tried tugging, but his grip remained firm. And he hadn't taken his eyes off her. He hadn't even blinked. She had a sudden impression that he wasn't even seeing her.

Shaking it off, she said, "If I could have my hand..."

"Come. We will have to talk."

Before she could protest, he was drawing her toward the library doors.

"Not here. First we will have dinner in my suite at the hotel," he said.

"No," A.J. said. Out of the corner of her eye, she could see that Sam had risen from behind his pot. "We won't be meeting at your hotel. We can meet here."

"At my hotel," Girard insisted. "Now that you work for me—"

A.J. dug in her heels. "But I don't work for you, Mr. LaBrecque."

"Nonsense. Your firm has agreed to my terms."

"No—"

"A.J., there you are." Jamison walked toward them with Rodney hot on his trail. "Margery said you'd stepped out here. I see you've met your new client."

"No." Then enunciating very clearly, she said, "Mr. LaBrecque is not my client."

All four men stared at her.

Satisfied that she had their undivided attention, she said, "Pierre Rabaut is my client. I will continue to represent him until he releases me."

"Just one moment, A.J." Her uncle stepped forward as Girard LaBrecque's grip tightened on her hand. "I have promised the LaBrecques that you will represent LaBrecque International. Rodney has notified Mr. Rabaut of that through his previous attorney."

A.J. met his eyes squarely. "You failed to notify me."

"You work for me." Jamison and Girard spoke in different accents in unison.

"No. I do not work for either of you." She pinned the older LaBrecque with a look. "And I want my hand back."

"Papa!"

Girard LaBrecque blinked at the same moment that he freed her fingers.

She gave the younger LaBrecque a brief nod. "Thank you." Then she turned to the other men. "I'm working for Mr. Rabaut. And to make sure that this doesn't cause a conflict of interest for the firm, Uncle Jamison, you will find my resignation on your desk on Monday."

Then turning on her heel, she walked away. Sam was at her side before she'd taken three strides. In another moment, they were in the hall heading toward the foyer.

"Have I told you that I like your style, counselor?" he asked.

"You're a minority of one," she said just as Sweeney stopped them at the door.

"A messenger just brought these," he said, handing them two envelopes.

A.J. glanced down at the pristine whiteness of the envelope, the neatly scripted handwriting.

The moment they were out in the hall, Sam opened his and read it. "We're meeting the kidnappers tomorrow at noon in Central Park."

9

"WHERE ARE WE HEADED NOW?"

The question came over the intercom of the limousine, but A.J. recognized it as the same one that was dancing around in her own mind. That first rush of freedom she'd felt as she'd left her uncle's office had faded a little as the elevator had sped her downward to the first floor. She'd resigned from Hancock, Potter and King. She might never be welcome in her aunt and uncle's home again. Where, indeed, was she headed now?

"The Willoughby." Sam reached for her hand. "You do want to stop back there, right?"

"Yes." She glanced at her watch. It was nearly seven. Claire would be waiting for the skirt, and she might have had a very long wait if Sam hadn't remembered.

"Are you all right?" Sam asked.

For a moment, she tightened her grip on his hand. "I think so. My future—it's like a blank slate."

He smiled at her. "You'll figure out just what to write on it."

No one had ever had that simple, clear faith in her before. And she *would* figure out her future. Part of it was sitting right in front of her, and she was going to have to figure out what to do about it.

"Well?" Sam asked. "Aren't you going to open it?"

"Hmmm?"

"The envelope. Mine's an invitation. We'd better check to see if we're invited to the same party."

A.J. turned the envelope over and slipped out the message. "'If you wish to see Pierre Rabaut again, your presence is required in Central Park at noon tomorrow. You know what to bring.' And there's a map."

"Mine reads the same. I think I know the spot on the map. It's over by the old stables. They're not used for horses anymore, and the area near there off the bridle path is fairly secluded."

"This is a very fancy ransom note," A.J. said, turning it over in her hand.

"Odd that they don't ask outright that we bring the necklace. Of course, we can't be positive that you and I are the only ones invited. But..."

"What?" A.J. asked.

"I need to think for a minute," Sam said.

A.J. watched as he leaned back against the seat and closed his eyes. Her own eyes narrowed. The detective at work, she supposed, but it looked a lot like he was copping a nap.

Turning, she gazed out the window of the limo. The last thing she wanted to do right now was think. On one corner, a man played a fiddle while a generous pedestrian dropped a bill into his open violin case. On another, a man wearing gold chains and mirrored sunglasses hawked a selection of purses lying on a blanket at his feet. Down the street, another man in shabby clothes just sat, waiting for the generosity of strangers.

As the limousine turned down a side street to wend its way toward the West Side, A.J. fixed her gaze back on Sam. The first time she'd seen him, she'd thought that he was homeless—a tramp. And even then, she hadn't been able to stop thinking about him, just as she couldn't now.

It was so easy to imagine what they'd done only a little

over an hour ago right here in the limousine, just as it was easy to recall what she'd felt while they'd been hiding on the terrace in her aunt's fake forest. His hands had been on her then. Just thinking about it brought the sensations back. She wanted them on her again.

"Sam?"

Without opening his eyes, he held up a hand.

Was he shushing her? A.J. frowned at him as he continued to ignore her. Whatever he was doing, his mind was clearly not focused on what hers was focused on—another bout of wild, hot sex in a limo. Her frown deepened as she glanced down at the skirt. Maybe it was losing its power. With three women all sharing it on the same day, it was certainly getting a workout. Fingering the hem, she studied it for a moment. Was it even the right skirt?

In her mind, she pictured Samantha taking it out of her closet that morning. Then she'd modeled her own Bloomingdale's version while she'd been waiting for Samantha to get home to switch skirts with her. They hadn't made a mistake then, she was sure.

Almost. Quickly, she reviewed the events of the evening. The skirt seemed to have affected Girard LaBrecque. The man had been glued to her hand. On the other hand, it hadn't drawn Sam to her earlier in the limousine. She was the one who'd put the moves on him. And it certainly hadn't influenced her uncle or her cousin to take her side when she'd insisted on representing Pierre. The bottom line was that she'd originally worn the skirt to ensure her future at Hancock, Potter and King, and now that future had ceased to exist.

And Claire was waiting for the real skirt right now!

As if on cue, the limousine pulled up to the curb.

"We're here," she said to Sam as the driver opened the door.

His eyes opened immediately. "Change into something comfortable. Do you own anything like shorts and sneakers?"

"Sure...but I thought we were—"

He smiled at her. "Oh, we'll get to that and more."

Her hand was already reaching for the door, but the man had moves—not slow and easy at all. Before she could blink, he'd slid her close and his mouth took hers. A wave of shimmering heat started where their mouths were joined and moved through her right down to her toes. She felt as if she were simply being absorbed particle by particle into him. The intensity, the intimacy of it stunned her. When he released her, she was sure her bones had melted.

"I promised you that I was going to make love to you slow and easy. But I want to take care of some business first. Okay?"

"'Kay," she managed, then prayed that her legs would hold her as he drew her out of the limousine.

They got to the front door at the same moment that Mrs. Higgenbotham alighted from a taxi with Antoine and Cleo. A.J. studied Cleo. The poodle looked like A.J. felt. A little shell-shocked, but happy. Antoine looked...like the cat who'd caught the canary. And Mrs. H. looked...like she'd just lost her best friend.

A.J. waited until Sam had ushered them all into the lobby of the Willoughby.

"How did the star-crossed lovers fare?" Franco opened one eye from his deck chair where he was catching the last slants of sun through the skylight.

The dogs nuzzled each other, and Mrs. Higgenbotham sighed. Even her caftan seemed to hang around her in dejected folds.

"Problem?" A.J. asked.

Mrs. H. shook her head. "No. Yes. I mean...my Cleo and

this..." She waved a hand at Antoine. "They're meant to be together. Dr. Fielding is positive that Cleo and Antoine have been drawn together by the stars."

"I'm putting my money on the skirt," Franco said.

"What are you talking about?" A.J. asked.

"A simple case of logical deduction," Franco explained, waving his hands in the air and sending dust motes swirling. "You three girls have been wearing that skirt, and you have been walking Cleo. She's been rubbing herself up against it constantly. Ergo, she has found her true love, thus fulfilling the legend of the skirt!"

"Well." Mrs. Higgenbotham blinked. "I'm pretty sure that Dr. Fielding wouldn't agree, Franco. He took Cleo and this...individual...through several past life regressions. And it seems that Cleo and Antoine have been looking for each other for at least three centuries. That's as far back as he had time to go. He's very anxious to go back to the time of the Pharaohs because he has a hunch it all started there. I'm to bring them back tomorrow. He's going to write a book about them."

"He'd be better off writing a book about that skirt," Franco said.

"I'll just bet he wants to write a book," A.J. said with a frown. "I'm going to have a little chat with him. If he intends to use Cleo and Antoine for research purposes, he's going to compensate you for your time. Instead of raking in a couple of hundred dollars an hour, he can start shelling it out."

"Oh." Mrs. Higgenbotham's expression brightened for the first time since she'd alighted from the taxi. "I love the way your mind works, dear. Maybe I won't have to sue Antoine's owner. Not that I really want to anymore. I mean I want Cleo to be happy. But they'll probably kick her out of the kennel club."

"Look on the bright side," Sam said. "She won't want to hang out there all that much now that she has Antoine."

"True." Mrs. Higgenbotham's smile blossomed even more brightly. "And if Cleo resigns from the kennel club, that will help to settle my other lawsuit, won't it, A.J.?"

"Yes, I think that might go a long way toward solving that problem."

"Good." Mrs. H. waved a hand and began to move toward the elevator. "I hate legal stuff. It's all so confusing."

A.J. followed the parade, being careful to avoid Mrs. H.'s billowing caftan.

THE MOMENT A.J. let herself into the apartment, the clock struck seven. "Claire," she called as she started to unzip the skirt. By the time she had it off, Claire was hurrying into the living room.

"You made it!"

"Sorry, I was almost late. It's a long story. There's only one problem. I'm not sure this is the right skirt."

"What do you mean?"

"Remember, there were two skirts in my closet this morning—the real one that I wore yesterday and my knockoff. Samantha wore the skirt that she thought was the real one today, then traded with me this afternoon. But I think there might have been a mix-up. It didn't seem to work the same way today."

Claire removed her own knockoff skirt and they held them up together. "Do they look the same to you?"

A.J. studied them. For the life of her, she couldn't tell the difference. "It's too dark in here. Let's go into Samantha's room. It has the best light."

But that didn't seem to help either. The skirts even felt the same when she rubbed the material between her fingers. "What do you think?"

"The one you were wearing seems to have more of a sheen to it. Why don't you think it's the real one?"

"Disaster struck at my aunt and uncle's cocktail party."

"Did you have a fight with the cute detective?"

"No." A.J. felt a blush stealing into her cheeks. "No, it's nothing like that. In fact, we're...great. You know, I think you're right. This one must be the real skirt."

Claire laid the skirt she held on Samantha's bed, then put on the one A.J. handed her. "How do I look?"

A.J. took her hand and squeezed it. "Nervous."

"I guess that's better than nauseous."

The moment that Claire left, A.J. raced to her room, dragged on shorts and exchanged her halter top for a T-shirt. A quick glance in the mirror triggered an attack of nerves in her stomach. At least Claire had a fifty-fifty chance of wearing the real skirt. She, on the other hand, was entirely on her own.

THE LAST PLACE IN THE WORLD she'd expected Sam to bring her was the rooftop of his family's hotel. They'd taken a private elevator, and then Sam had excused himself to change his clothes.

She'd heard of rooftop gardens on Manhattan buildings, but someone here knew what they were doing. A penthouse apartment took up one corner with its own private patio and garden complete with a fountain. But the greenery continued past the private corner. Flowers bloomed in urns and pots, filling the evening air with their scents.

And then she saw the basketball court, smack in the middle of the roof. The baskets themselves were on wheels and held down by sandbags. Bleachers lined one side of the court, and picnic tables stood in a row on the other.

"My family loves basketball," Sam said.

"I see," she said, turning to study him. He'd changed into

faded denim shorts, an equally faded gray T-shirt and just looking at him made her mouth water. He began to dribble the basketball he was holding. "Wanna play some hoop?"

She glanced at the court and then at him. "You're serious."

"Romanos never joke about basketball. It helps me to mull things over. Whenever I'm particularly stumped by a case, shooting some baskets helps."

"Really? I thought that quick nap you got in the limo might have helped."

He grinned at her. "It wasn't a nap. I slipped into a dream state so that my subconscious could play around with the puzzle pieces. That's my number one strategy. Basketball is number two. Care to join me?"

She held out her hands and caught the ball neatly when he shot it to her.

"Have you ever played before?"

"You just have to get it to go through that little hoop, right?"

"Right. Go ahead and take a few practice shots."

A.J. went to the free throw line, took a minute to aim the shot, then tossed the ball. The silence with which it slid through the net made her smile. The look on Sam's face made her laugh.

"You *have* played before," he said.

"You think?" she asked as her second ball sank into the net.

"Do it again."

She did. And the delight streamed through him. If he hadn't already fallen in love with her he would have right then. He wanted to tell her. But he'd promised himself that he would give her time. He understood the kind of courage it had taken for her to make the break she had tonight. And he thought he knew the kind of pain that she was suffering because of it. Family was family, after all. The last thing he wanted to do was add to the pressures that he was sure she was feeling.

"Where did you play?" he asked.

She sank another ball before she answered. "In prep school. It was a way to fit in and be accepted."

Sam felt the surge of anger and banked it. She shouldn't have to work to fit in. He was going to have to show her that.

"I can see you're aces at the free throw line. How about a little one on one?"

"Thought you'd never ask," A.J. said as she shot the ball at him.

By the time he pivoted, she was on him, matching him step for step as he headed toward the other end of the court. If he hadn't had a good twelve inches on her, she would have blocked his shot. A smile split his face as she grabbed the ball from under the net and dodged neatly around him.

His legs were longer and he easily passed her, but just as he turned and threw out an arm to block her shot, she darted under it. He heard the swish before he could turn around to see the ball fall through the basket.

"You're good," he said as she grabbed the rebound and began to dribble.

"Yep. How's the mulling going?"

He cut across her, snatching the ball just as it was about to meet her palm. By the time he pivoted, she was at his side, and she stuck there as he raced down the court. He was holding the ball easily out of her reach when she rammed her shoulder into his chest and snagged it from his hands. Before he could recover from the shock, she'd streaked her way past him. The ball hit the backboard this time and wobbled on the rim before it sank.

When he reached her, she was dribbling the ball and looking at him with a cocky tilt to her chin. He didn't think he could have wanted her more.

"That was a foul back there," he said.

"I didn't hear anyone call it."

Eyes narrowed, he studied her for a minute. "You're serious about this game, aren't you?"

"I'm always serious about basketball."

"Let's play," Sam said.

And they did. He lost track of the time as they raced together up and down the court. He should have known the first time he saw those legs that she'd be good on a basketball court. Long and strong, they took two steps to his one. Every single time he turned she was there.

Of course, he couldn't throw the same kind of blocks on her that he used on his brothers, or that she used on him. But other than that, they were pretty evenly matched. What A.J. lacked in height, she made up for in quickness—and downright sneakiness.

What a woman!

He was as winded as she was when they finally paused midcourt to catch a breath.

"Did you come up with the solution yet, Sherlock?"

Sam threw back his head and laughed. "You're a lot tougher to deal with than Watson."

"Count on it."

Throwing his arm around her, he dribbled the ball with his free hand and said, "Let's see if it worked. Let's mull this over together. Are you game?"

"Lead the way. I'm sure I'll get the hang of it."

Sam had no doubt about it as he began to walk down the court, bouncing the ball as he went. "First puzzle piece—we have two fake necklaces and the real one seems to be missing."

A.J. nodded.

"Puzzle piece number two—the bearded man. He keeps turning up like a bad penny. First, he accosted Pierre as soon as he left the museum. Then he tried to snatch your purse, or perhaps you. And he followed you later, to get the purse and/or you again. And he helped kidnap Pierre."

At the end of the court, he turned and began to pace back to the other end with A.J. at his side. "Puzzle piece number three—the break-in at Pierre's apartment. Was it the work of the bearded man or the LaBrecques? Or someone else?"

"The older one, Girard, is certainly fixated on Pierre."

"And you."

"They've got some financial need, because they're expanding their markets, and if the necklace was stolen, they could collect the insurance. Girard also has some issues about the fact that Marie once loved Pierre."

"That kind of possessiveness suggests the possibility that Girard's elevator doesn't go to the top floor."

"So he might think he can destroy Pierre and collect on the necklace in one fell swoop." A.J. stopped short in her tracks. "I just remembered. There's something I forgot about until just now. Bob Carter told me that a few months ago Pierre came into an inheritance and the will was going to be contested. It may be nothing, but the timing struck me. It was three months ago that he flew to Rheims for Marie's funeral. There might be a connection."

"What are you thinking?"

"I'm not sure. The attorney that Pierre talked to is going to call me in the morning. But what if Marie left something to Pierre in her will? That might be enough to fire up some thoughts of revenge."

Letting the ball go, Sam lifted her and swung her around in his arms. "You're brilliant. I told you this mulling works. Why don't you give that French policeman a call in the morning and see if there's any gossip?"

A.J. glanced at her watch. "I don't have to wait. He said I can call anytime."

HOLDING THE BALL between both of his palms, Sam listened to A.J. sweet-talk a French policeman. His fluency in Italian allowed him to follow the gist of her conversation. The man was going to see if he could find out what was in Marie Bernard LaBrecque's will. It hadn't been made public, but the man had a cousin who had connections to someone who worked for the attorney.

A.J. was smiling, laughing with the man on the other end of the line. He might have been jealous if it weren't for the fact that the policeman was in Rheims and Sam was right here with A.J.

No, not A.J., he decided. It was Arianna who was making the phone call. He wondered if she was aware of the change. She didn't like to reveal her softer side, didn't like to admit she had one. No wonder with that family of hers.

The moment she hung up the phone, Sam tossed the basketball away and moved toward her.

"He's going to call me back as soon as he has something."

Smiling, he took her hands in his. "I want to thank you for mulling with me. You're good at it."

"But we haven't really solved anything yet. And we haven't found Pierre."

Sam sighed. "I don't remember Watson being this hard on Holmes."

"Watson was a wimp, and he missed most of the good clues."

"I have a feeling—call it P.I. instinct—that between your French policeman and the little party in Central Park tomorrow, we're going to get ourselves a plate load of clues. In the meantime, I want to try strategy three."

She eyed him suspiciously. "What is it?"

"Well, I've never tried it before, so it would be experimental. But since you've pointed out to me that slipping into a dream state and playing hoop have not produced satisfactory results, I'm desperate."

Her eyes narrowed slightly. "And just what is this experimental strategy?"

He gripped her chin and tilted it up. "I want to make love to you."

The words alone were enough to have the need building inside of her. But she cocked her head to one side. "And what makes you think that would work?"

"Elementary, my dear Watson," he murmured as he began to nibble at her lips. "Haven't you ever come up with the solution to a particular problem when you least expected it? When you were in the middle of something else entirely and you weren't thinking about it at all?"

"Sure. All the time." His mouth was working its magic on her shoulder and her skin felt hot and icy at the same time. She was having to struggle to focus on the thread of their conversation, but she thought she had it. "You think we'll figure out the solution if we have sex?"

Because he couldn't resist, he took the lobe of her ear between his teeth. "Not sex, Arianna. I'm going to make love with you."

"My name is A.J." She struggled to hold on to the thought as his mouth continued to make its way to hers. But just when she thought he would kiss her again, he drew back a little.

"But you're Arianna too. And making love is different than having sex. I'm going to show you."

Please, she thought, struggling to focus. "Do you think Sherlock ever used this technique with Watson?"

He laughed then, framing her face with his hands. "Hey, you never know. Are you game?"

Wrapping her arms around him, she brought her mouth to

his ear and tried a little magic of her own. "I thought you'd never ask."

"C'mon then," he said as he drew her with him to the penthouse apartment that took up one corner of the roof. But he didn't take her inside. Instead, he stopped the moment she stepped up onto the patio.

"There," he said. "I thought it might work."

"What?" she asked.

"When you stand on that step, you're just the right height for kissing. Don't move."

A.J. waited while he disappeared into the penthouse. A moment later, music filled the air. Before he returned, she had time to notice candles burning on a small table and wine chilling in a bucket. He must have set the scene when he'd changed his clothes. The sweetness of the gesture moved her.

She was in love with Sam Romano. The joy, the scariness of it, shot through her like champagne bubbles. She wanted to shout it from the rooftop. But she couldn't. It had to be the last thing Sam wanted to hear.

And then he was back on the patio, moving down the step, and turning toward her. He said nothing, just took her hands and lifted them one at a time to kiss her palms. Then he raised his hands to frame her face before he brought his mouth to hers. The kiss was so soft, so gentle.

"Perfect," he murmured.

A.J. felt herself melting inside.

"I WANT YOU," Sam whispered against her lips. Forever. The word had slipped into his mind the moment he'd stepped back out onto the patio and seen her standing with the lights of the Manhattan skyline at her back. He wanted her with him forever. Even as the shock of it moved through him, he knew it was true.

Forever. The word repeated in his head as he took his

mouth on a lazy journey along her jaw to the silky, soft skin beneath her ear. Her scent was darker there, lighter at the hollow of her throat. Bathed in moonlight, she'd looked like the statue of a goddess, her hair silver, her skin as pale and delicate as porcelain.

But she was warm, human. He ran his hands along the line of her throat to her shoulders. And fragile. There was such strength in her that he forgot how delicate she was. And how small. Even standing on the step above him, her head barely came up to his nose.

For one moment he brought his mouth back to hers and feasted. Her flavors poured into him until need began to sharpen.

Drawing back while he still could, he lifted her T-shirt over her head and found the scrap of lace and silk beneath. So arousing. Then keeping his eyes on hers, he began to discover her with his hands. Slowly. Using just his fingertips, he traced her collarbone, then found her breasts, the line of her ribs, the narrow waist. "I've waited so long to do this," he said.

Forever.

PLEASURE, RIBBONS OF IT streamed through her as her mind fogged and her vision grayed. This was so different from what they'd shared in the limo. In the place of fire, there was a slowly building flame. Still, it was hot enough to have melted her bones.

There were so many sensations to savor. The soft brush of his fingertips over the top of her breast. The light pressure of his thumb circling the nipple. The sure stroke of those long fingers as they moved down her ribs to her waist. No one had ever touched her this way—as if he knew exactly what would please her. No one had ever looked at her this way—as if he was determined to learn all of her secrets.

She'd been waiting for someone to touch her like this... forever.

His hands moved lower to her hips and drew her closer. "Arianna."

Her arms moved around him and tangled in his hair. "No one calls me that."

She lost her train of thought as she felt the strength of his erection pressing into the softness of her stomach.

"No one but me, Arianna."

When he cupped her hips and lifted, she wrapped her legs around him. "No one but you," she murmured as she pressed her mouth to his throat.

THE WORDS DRUMMED THROUGH HIM as he carried her into the bedroom. Moonlight shone through the windows and pooled around the bed. Sam lowered them both onto it as carefully as he could. He wanted to go slowly and finish the gentle seduction he'd begun on the patio, but his control was on a thin leash. It stretched even thinner when she began to work at the fastenings of his clothes.

She was fast, and her hands were clever. The places she touched as she pushed his T-shirt out of the way—his waist, his chest, his throat, everywhere—flames licked along his skin. His body seemed to fascinate her as she worked the same magic with his shorts. He managed to salvage the foil packet while some sanity remained. In the rational part of his mind, he could have sworn she was two women—Arianna, the delicate goddess on the patio, and A.J., the siren who was luring him to the edge right now.

His mind was teeming with both of them—with every part of them that he could taste or touch. Unsnapping her shorts, he pulled them inch by inch down her legs, following the path with his mouth.

Arianna and A.J.—the words echoed in his mind. He loved both of them. Wanted both of them. Now.

Pressing her down into the mattress, he tore open the condom. Then her hands were there, sheathing him, driving him mad.

And then pulled her beneath him and rose above her.

"Only you."

He wasn't sure who said the words. He only knew that he was inside her at last. Their hands met, pressed palm against palm, and he linked his fingers with hers. Joined, they began to move as one—slowly at first and then in a growing speed until the world spun away and they knew only each other.

10

FOR A LONG TIME neither one of them spoke. There was so much that Sam wanted to tell her. Most of all he wanted to tell her that he loved her. But she wasn't ready to hear it.

Patience was something that he'd worked to instill in himself, but it was costing him with A.J. She'd been raised to look for Mr. Perfect—the man with the right background, education and portfolio. He had none of the above. Nevertheless, he was going to have her in his life. Permanently. All he needed was the right strategy.

When he began to lever himself off of her, she tightened her grip on him.

"Don't," she murmured.

"I move for this position instead, counselor." He rolled so that she was lying on top of him, then eased her head into the crook of his shoulder. "Okay?"

"Mmmmmm."

As the silence settled over them again, the realization washed through him that he could have stayed just this way forever.

Finally, she lifted her head and looked into his eyes. "I don't think Holmes and Watson ever did what we just did."

Sam hadn't thought he had the energy to laugh, but it seemed that he did. Reaching up, he tucked a strand of hair behind her ear. "Next, you'll be asking me if the strategy worked."

"Did it?" she asked.

Just then her stomach growled.

"I move for a postponement," he said. "We can talk after I feed you."

THEY PICNICKED BY CANDLELIGHT, sitting cross-legged on the bed. Jazz, low and bluesy, flowed out of some speakers, and they ate cold, tangy chicken, mellow brie, and drank champagne, bubbly and dry. Sam's cousin Lucy had prepared the meal for them, and A.J. was sure it was delicious. But she could barely taste it. Her thoughts were too filled with Sam. It nearly overwhelmed her that, in the midst of everything, he had taken the time to give her romance.

He sat across from her smiling, his eyes so intent on hers, as if he was looking at everything he ever wanted. She felt one minute as if they had been lovers forever, and the next as if they had never been intimate and he was just wooing her.

She wanted to tell him what she was feeling. More than that, she wanted to tell him that she loved him. But fear stopped her. On the night that she'd lost so much of what she'd always thought she wanted, she wanted to hold on to this.

"More champagne?" Sam asked.

"No," she said. And knowing that she was taking the coward's way out, she said, "Don't you think it's time you told me if the latest strategy brought us any closer to finding Pierre?"

Sam was reaching for her hand when her cell phone rang.

"Who would be calling?" she asked as she reached for her purse and pulled it out.

"Your French cop, I'll bet."

And it was. He was so excited that it took all of her concentration to get what he was saying to her. When she hung up, she boiled it down for Sam. "Marie Bernard LaBrecque left the Abelard necklace to Pierre Rabaut in her will. And according to my French cop, there hasn't been any gossip about it. His cousin's wife's friend has been sworn to secrecy."

Sam's brows rose. "Evidently it's not a very binding vow. What else did he learn?"

"The LaBrecques are contesting the will by claiming that Marie was not in her right mind. They'll have witnesses, but the family attorney is not hopeful. She was evidently quite lucid when she talked to him about her wishes." A.J. smiled at him. "That too is a secret."

SAM'S MIND WAS RACING. "If Pierre owns the real one—or will own it as soon as the courts give it to him—then why would he steal it?"

"I've been telling you all along that he didn't."

Moving from the bed, Sam began to pace. "There's a fake one in the display case at the museum and a fake one in your purse. And the real one is..."

"In the museum," A.J. said.

Sam turned to her. "You're stubborn, you're loyal and you just might be right."

Then he reached to pull her from the bed and swing her around in a circle. "You might be absolutely right. From the moment I saw Pierre climb through that skylight, I've been sure that he stole the necklace. I haven't had the faith in him that you've had all along. I'm betting—you're right—that the necklace is still in the museum, just not in the display case. That would certainly explain his note to me. Things aren't always as they appear to be. Pierre only appeared to steal the necklace." Setting her down, he kissed her hard, then released her. "Thanks."

She smiled up at him. "We still don't have all the answers. We don't know where Pierre is."

"Time to get into mulling mode again. I think I'm coming

to prefer strategy number three." He grinned at her as he pulled off her T-shirt. "Let's give it another try."

A.J. DRESSED TO THE SOUND of Debussy. She'd never tried it before, but then she'd never started her day showering with Sam. It was something that she wanted to make a daily habit, and she was going to have to tell him. Just as soon as she figured out how. Moving out onto the patio, she sat down on the step to mull over the best strategy.

"Hi."

A.J. jumped up and whirled to find herself staring into two pairs of very curious eyes. She judged the two girls to be in their teens, and both of them had Sam's dark good looks. They were also both carrying loaded trays. "Hi."

"Are we disturbing you?" the younger one asked. "Sam called down and told us we could come up, but—"

"You're not disturbing me. Let me help you." Taking the tray from the girl, she set it on the table.

"I'm Grace and she's Lucy," the older girl explained as she set down her tray. "We're Sam's cousins. My mom couldn't be here because she's visiting my older brother Nick in Boston."

"I'm A.J."

"I love your name," Lucy said. "Initials sound so professional. What do you think of L.C.?"

"*I* think it sounds too much like *Elsie*. Lucy hates her name," Grace explained.

"I do not."

"Then why are you always threatening to change it?" Grace asked.

"Time out, girls." A tall man appeared around the potted plants that screened the patio. "I'm Sam's big brother, Tony."

He was bigger than Sam, A.J. noted, and he had a generous share of the good looks that she was beginning to believe were embedded in the Romano genes.

The thought barely had time to form in her mind when Tony enveloped her in a hug. "Welcome to Henry's Place." A second later, he stepped back to study her briefly. "Andrew said you were pretty, but pretty doesn't do you justice."

"Sam said you were beautiful," Lucy said.

Tony grinned then. "He's right, but don't anyone tell Sam I said that."

"Too late." Sam appeared in the doorway, a cell phone pressed to his ear. "You all can go ahead. I'll be with you in a minute."

And go ahead they did. Before she could blink, A.J. found herself seated between Lucy and Grace at the table with her plate piled high with a fluffy omelet, sausages and slices of melon. She was sure that she must have politely refused some of it, but everyone had seemed to be talking at once.

Family meals at her aunt and uncle's had never been like this. They'd sat yards away from one another, and she couldn't recall anyone ever laughing.

"Eat," Tony said as he passed her a mug of steaming coffee. "Lucy made the omelet. You'll hurt her feelings if you don't at least sample."

Aware of Lucy's wide brown eyes on her, A.J. dug in. The flavors danced on her tongue. "Delicious. I loved the picnic you packed for Sam too."

"She's going to be a Cordon Bleu chef one day," Sam said as he joined them.

"I'm going to be a lawyer," Grace said.

A.J. turned to her and read the unspoken question in her eyes. "Maybe we could talk about that someday."

Grace's smile bloomed as the conversation bubbled up around them again. As she made her way happily through her omelet, A.J. heard the talk veer from the restaurant's latest menu to Pierre's disappearance, and then on to gardening and sports. A.J. wasn't sure how anyone could eat and get so many subjects covered at the same time. Questions shot from all directions, and forks were used frequently to emphasize a point.

"There's a basketball tournament on Sunday. Could you play?"

In the sudden silence that followed the question, A.J. glanced up to see that Tony was pointing at her with his fork.

"Me?" she asked.

"Sam told us that you beat him," Lucy said with awe in her voice. "Is that true?"

"She wiped her plate with me," Sam said.

Tony shot her a charming grin. "It's just a little family rivalry—the Romanos versus the McGarriety's. They run the health club we refer our guests to. It would seriously damage the family honor if we lost."

"It would damage Tony's bank account more," Sam said in a low tone. "I think he and Tim McGarriety are risking more than honor."

Tony waved his fork. "That's beside the point."

Everyone was looking at her now, A.J. realized. She read determination in Tony's eyes, wonder in Grace's and Lucy's, and pride in Sam's. "Sure."

A collective sigh of relief went around the table.

"Okay," Sam said, rising and taking her hand. "Mission accomplished. You can get back to running the hotel. A.J. and I have detective work to do."

Still, A.J. noted that it still took them five full minutes, most of it spent in hugging, to make it to the private elevator.

"Your family," she began as the doors slid shut, "they're—" How could she tell him that they made her feel as if she belonged? "You're very lucky."

Sam grinned at her and squeezed her hand. "Yeah. I think I'll keep them."

"I have a favor to ask," A.J. said as he whistled a taxi to the curb. "I want to stop at my apartment on the way and get the skirt. I figure we'll need all the luck we can get with these kidnappers."

Tipping her chin up Sam gave her a quick hard kiss. "I like the way your mind works, Watson."

A.J. AND SAM ARRIVED at the entrance to the park with barely a moment to spare. The sun was bright, the air hot. Sunbathers lazed on blankets, and strollers and joggers jockeyed for position on the path. She had plenty of time to take it all in because Sam had been deep in the mulling zone ever since they'd left the Willoughby.

Getting the skirt had been trickier than she'd thought.

If it was the right skirt. A.J. glanced down at it. She was almost sure it was. But each time she replayed the scene that had occurred in her apartment, her conviction wavered.

She and Samantha had entered the apartment at the same time, and she couldn't help but notice two things—Samantha was wearing the skirt and glowing.

"Well, well, well. Do I take it the skirt worked its magic?"

"Maybe." Samantha glanced down at it. "I'd better wear it today, even though people are beginning to think I don't have anything else."

"But we don't know if that's the skirt," Claire said, stepping out of her bedroom.

A.J. glanced at Claire. She was glowing too.

Samantha frowned down at the one she was wearing. "I changed into a skirt that was lying on my bed."

"Yeah, well, there were two black skirts in my closet yesterday morning—yours and my copy. Did you take the right one?" A.J. asked.

"Let's compare," Samantha said.

A.J. looked at Claire and knew that they were both recalling the scene in Samantha's bedroom when they'd held the skirts up to the light to figure out which was which. Claire had worn the one that they'd decided was the *real* skirt. Had they been wrong?

A.J. tugged down the waist of the skirt she was wearing and quickened her pace. In the end, they hadn't been able to figure it out. Samantha had decided to wear the one she had on because it had worked for her. A.J. had changed into the one Claire had worn last night because it had obviously worked for her. Now, all she could do was hope that the one she was wearing was the real one. For a meeting with kidnappers and possible jewel thieves, a girl needed a little magic.

Not to mention the fact that she needed it with the man walking next to her who was still mulling. When she had to push Sam onto the grass to avoid an imminent collision with a little boy on a bike, she decided a little cross-examination was called for.

"If I promise you immunity from prosecution, will you tell me what's bothering you?"

"I'm just mulling."

"Me too. Let's mull together. I thought the will was good news. It certainly explains a lot. At least now we know why Girard LaBrecque hates Pierre, and it gives him a fresh motive for wanting to get rid of your godfather."

"But it raises almost as many questions as it answers. If Pierre owns the necklace, why did he break into the museum in the first place? And why did Marie Bernard LaBrecque leave it to him?"

A.J. studied him for a minute. "Maybe she loved him. Maybe she regretted staying with LaBrecque."

"Or she felt guilty because she couldn't bring herself to give up the life her family wanted for her."

A.J. reached out and took his hand. "Maybe both. Maybe we don't know the whole story."

"One thing I do know. I don't want you to go with me to the meeting. It's too dangerous. I want you to wait here."

A.J.'s brows rose. So this was what he'd been brooding about. "Not on your life. I have an invitation, and Pierre's my client."

He gripped her arms with his hands. "I've already sent Luis and Tyrone to the spot to cover us, but I know that section of the park. They won't be able to get close enough to take an accurate shot if something goes wrong. I don't have a good feeling about this, and my instincts are usually right."

"So are mine," she said, taking a step closer. "Get this straight. You are not going to get rid of me. I'm sticking to you like glue."

She didn't protest when he closed what was left of the distance between them and covered her mouth with his. The kiss was just what she remembered—hard, fierce, demanding. She responded immediately, softening, opening.

Walkers continued to stroll by. Not even the squeal of a child or a long, low wolf whistle could penetrate the world that they were creating together. She slid her hands up his arms to his shoulders and pressed herself closer until she could feel the hard lines of his body. She wanted him to know that she wasn't going anywhere. She wasn't like Marie LaBrecque, nor was she like Isabelle Sheridan. She wasn't going to send him away, nor was she going to give him half a loaf. Instead, she was going to be like Cleo—absolutely determined to get her man.

And she would wear that skirt, every day if she had to, until he figured it out.

When Sam drew back, his breathing was as ragged as hers.

"Feeling better now?" she asked.

He laughed as he rested his forehead against hers. "Was that your idea of therapy?"

"Works for me."

"Me too," Sam said, then sighed. "When we get there, I want you right by my side the entire time."

"You've got that too." And maybe eventually, she would wear him down to the point he'd believe it.

SAM LED A.J. down a small incline to a huge elm tree that had been drawn and marked with an X. The stables which were no longer in use stood a short distance away. There was also a wooded area about a hundred yards to the left that he was keeping an eye on, and an old stone bridge farther off to the right. Either place offered some cover, and he imagined that both Tyrone and Luis were making good use of it.

He had to admit that the kidnappers had chosen wisely. The spot wasn't entirely private, but it was as close as a person could get on a summer day in Central Park. He could just make out the old stables through the trees, and it was from that direction that he first spotted the LaBrecques, Girard with his cane and Bernard walking beside him.

Sam squeezed A.J.'s hand as they started down the incline. "Just stay close. I don't see any sign of Pierre, so we're going to have to play this by ear."

Neither of the LaBrecques spoke until they stopped beneath the tree. Then Girard spoke to A.J. "Where is Rabaut?"

"That's what we want to know," Sam said.

"We didn't come here to play games. Where is Pierre Rabaut?" Girard LaBrecque raised his cane and sliced the air.

It caught the edge of Sam's shoulder before he had a chance to dodge. Recovering, he drew A.J. back a step and edged himself in front of her.

"Papa." Bernard stepped forward and laid a hand on the

older man's arm. "I apologize for my father, Ms. Potter and Mr...."

"Romano. I work for Sterling Security, the firm you hired to protect the necklace."

Bernard frowned. "Why are you here?"

"Ms. Potter and I both received invitations saying that if we came here at noon we would find Pierre Rabaut. So where is he?"

"Enough of this! I demand that you turn over Rabaut," Girard said, pounding his cane. "I should have killed him years ago."

"Papa." Bernard spoke sternly to his father, then turned to A.J. again.

"I'm sorry. My father has not been himself since my mother died. We're here today because we received invitations too."

"Rabaut is supposed to be here with the necklace he stole," Girard said.

"But he didn't steal it," A.J. said.

For a moment, Girard said nothing. He merely stared at A.J. with the same entranced look on his face that Sam had seen on the terrace the night before.

"You look so much like her...." His voice trailed off for a moment. "So very much like her. Stubborn. Marie didn't believe he had stolen the necklace either. He hadn't, of course. But it was easy to arrange for him to be found with the necklace on him, and even when he was thrown in jail, she believed in him."

"Papa, that's enough," Bernard said.

Girard raised his cane, and for a moment Sam was sure he was going to strike his son. "Don't interrupt. I want to tell Ms. Potter."

A look passed between the two men, and the younger one backed down.

When Girard turned back to A.J., his voice was calmer. "Marie was young and stubborn. She was going to be loyal to Pierre, just as you are determined to be loyal to him. So we came to an agreement." He took a step toward A.J. "You are young, headstrong, and we will come to an agreement too if you wish to see Pierre alive again. I assured your uncle that you would change your mind about working for us."

The old man's tone was calm, matter-of-fact. He might have been talking about the weather. But it was Girard's eyes that had the fear washing over Sam. He'd gotten a hint of it on the balcony, but it was clear to him now that Girard La-Brecque was mad. Had his wife's death pushed him over the edge or had it been the will? Maybe the roots of it had always been there.

He shifted his attention to Bernard. How long had the son been dealing with this and trying to keep up the façade? And what effect had it had on him?

Things are not always as they appear to be.

Sam could have cursed out loud when his fingers started tingling. Why hadn't his godfather just left him a note telling him that *nothing* was what it appeared to be!

Not even the kidnapping?

"What agreement did you make with Marie?" A.J. asked.

Good girl, Sam thought. Keep him talking. He had to think. Had Pierre set up the whole kidnapping? Sam ran the scene at the courthouse through his mind. The bearded man had clearly been after A.J. He'd taken off in his green van after the limo, but he could as easily have been chasing it as following it.

It was the two linebackers who'd come for Pierre.

Always do the unexpected.

Sam turned it over in his mind. Staging his own kidnapping would have been a good way for his godfather to keep himself safe, frustrate whoever was after him, and play a little game of his own. And if his hunch was correct, Pierre was close by right now.

It took more effort than he would have thought possible to keep himself from glancing up into the branches of the elm tree. But he couldn't afford to take his eyes off the two men in front of him.

"Marie agreed to go ahead with the marriage," Girard said. "She had been raised to marry me. I knew that she would come to her senses after a while. So I told her if she didn't marry me, I would have Rabaut killed."

"You would have killed him?" A.J. asked.

Girard shrugged. "I explained to Marie just how I would do it. Some poison slipped into the jail on his food tray—it would have been so simple to arrange. That was when she promised to marry me and stay with me—but she insisted I set Rabaut free and let him live. I agreed on the condition that he leave the country and that she never see him again. To seal our agreement, I gave her the Abelard necklace on the day we were married."

"You were besotted with her even then," Bernard said. "And she has brought ruin on this family."

"Don't speak of your mother that way!" The moment Girard raised his cane to his son, Sam knew exactly what A.J. would do. He made a grab for her as she rushed forward to shove Bernard out of the way, but his hand closed around air. Then the pain exploded at the side of his head.

"SAM!" Pushing herself away from Bernard, A.J. ran to where Sam had fallen and dropped to her knees. She saw blood on his temple, then heard him moan. She glared up at Girard. "Don't you dare hit him again. I'll testify to assault with a deadly weapon, and you'll find yourself in jail."

"Papa," said Bernard. "You handled this problem before. It's my turn now."

When A.J. saw Girard lower the cane, she turned to Bernard. The gun was the first thing she saw. Sun filtering through the branches of the tree glinted off the metal. Even then it took a moment to register that it was pointed at Sam and her. And then another moment for the fear to begin to build.

"I want the necklace, Ms. Potter," he said. "And then we are going for a little ride."

His voice was as calm as his father's had been. He might have been asking her to pass the salt. And his eyes... For the first time, she realized that he might be nearly as mad as his father. She had to think. And she had to keep him talking. "What necklace?"

"The one Pierre Rabaut walked down the front steps of the Grenelle Museum with on Thursday morning. Don't bother trying to deny it. I saw Pierre put it in your purse. I was there in a parked car across the street."

"*She* has the necklace?" his father asked.

"Yes," Bernard said softly. "And she's going to give it to me or I will put a bullet in Mr. Romano."

A.J. sprang to her feet and pulled her bag from her shoulder.

"That's right." Bernard held out his free hand.

Stall. Stall. The word pulsed in her mind. "How did you know that Pierre was going to take the necklace?"

"Because we had an agreement," Bernard said. "Father is not the only one in the family who knows how to make them. When Pierre showed up to claim the necklace, Father told him we were going to contest the will, that Mother wasn't in her right mind when she made it. The court case would have taken years to settle, so I offered your Mr. Rabaut a quicker way to get his inheritance. All he had to do was steal the necklace from the Grenelle Museum when it went on display. He would get the necklace that Mother wanted him to have, and I could collect the insurance money to finance the expansion of the vineyard. It was what you Americans call a win-win situation, no?"

"No," she said, taking a step away from Sam without moving any closer to Bernard. Sam's face was away from the LaBrecques, and she'd seen him open an eye. If she could keep Bernard's attention focused on herself, Sam might be able to make a move. "You were going to double-cross him. You hired that bearded man to mug him and take back the necklace, didn't you?"

"Very good, Ms. Potter. Perhaps my father was right to want to hire you to represent us. But you underestimate me. I hired the bearded man to kill Pierre Rabaut and bring me the necklace. I did not intend to make the same mistake that my father had by letting him live."

A.J. took another careful step to the side. It was a strategy she'd seen on the cop shows. Bernard couldn't keep the gun on both of them at once. Each step she took to get around Sam, she managed to widen the distance between herself and Bernard. "What about the hit-and-run driver? Wasn't that just overkill?"

"My father hired him. I hired my own man because I wanted the necklace. Once I have the money that the Abelard will bring, I will be able to make the necessary changes at LaBrecque International. Hurry, Ms. Potter. Or I'll shoot Mr. Romano in the back. I'm a very good shot."

There was a buzzing in her ears. Fear. She couldn't let it overpower her. A.J. took a step forward, then another, and felt the skirt inch its way up her legs.

The skirt. She'd completely forgotten about it. She took another step and felt it inch up again. "If you knew I had the necklace, why did you kidnap Pierre?"

All the while she was talking, A.J. tried to picture exactly what Samantha had done that day when she used the skirt on Tavish. She'd kept her eyes right on him. And she'd wiggled her hips.

"I didn't kidnap Pierre." It was fury she heard in his voice now. "He arranged for that little disappearance all by himself. Now he seems to have invited us here."

A.J. felt a lot of little puzzle pieces slip into place. But she didn't have time to think about them right now. She couldn't even blink. She was almost sure that she saw the gun waver a little in Bernard's hand. Stare. Step. Wiggle. Pause.

"When Pierre comes to rescue you, I will handle him myself."

Stare. Step. Wiggle.

Afterward, she wasn't quite sure of the exact sequence of events. There was a flash of light. That much she was sure of. It was bright enough that Bernard and his father raised hands to their eyes. A.J. launched herself at Bernard, grabbing his gun hand. Sam was right with her, going in low and hitting LaBrecque in the waist.

In her peripheral vision, she was almost sure she saw someone drop from the tree onto Girard.

Then the sound of the gun going off deafened her.

Her ears were still ringing when Luis and Tyrone were snapping handcuffs on the LaBrecques and Sam was holding her close. And she couldn't hear a thing that Pierre Rabaut said to her as he lifted her free hand and kissed it.

11

A.J. SANK ONTO A CHAIR that Andrew had cleared for her and selected a slice of the pizza he'd just ordered. Sam took a slice of pizza, but ignored the chair next to hers. They'd been at the police station for hours tying up loose ends. Andrew had suggested they all take a food break while he typed up Pierre's final statement. A.J. looked down at her pizza. She should be hungry, but nerves were still dancing in her stomach.

Sam was clearly annoyed with her. Not that it seemed to be affecting his appetite. Out of the corner of her eye, she watched him making his way through his slice of pizza as he paced back and forth between Andrew's desk and the window. He hadn't said more than a handful of words to her since they'd left the park. In fact, the only people who'd said less than Sam since they'd arrived at the precinct were the LaBrecques. They'd both clammed up and demanded attorneys the moment the police had arrived on the scene.

Uncle Jamison and Rodney had looked pretty grim when they'd arrived at the precinct, and her uncle had told her that he wanted to talk to her as soon as he was done with the LaBrecques. From the triumphant look on Rodney's face, she knew it wouldn't be good news. Pressing fingers to her temple, she tried to will away the headache that was beginning to build there.

"Okay, Pierre," Andrew said as he finished his slice of pizza and turned his attention back to his computer screen.

"You were at the point where you were telling me what you did with the jewels once you took them out of the display case."

"I want to read that before Pierre signs it," A.J. said, turning to focus her attention on the statement.

"Relax, counselor," Andrew said. "I told you that I'm not going to file charges against your client. Even though—" he held up a hand to silence her "—he shouldn't have staged his own kidnapping. And he shouldn't have stolen the Abelard necklace from the museum despite that it's probably his."

"I object to the word *stole.* My client never removed the necklace from the museum. He merely hid it in one of the heating ducts there for safekeeping until the matter of ownership could be determined by the courts."

"And I wasn't kidnapped. I just took a ride in the country with some friends," Pierre said.

A.J. beamed a smile at him. She loved a client who followed her instructions to the letter.

Andrew snorted. "Right. Just tell me what else I can put in this little story I'm typing up." Scrolling back, he continued. "This is what I've got so far. When you got the notice of Marie's death and your inheritance, you flew over for the funeral. After you arrived, the elder LaBrecque had murder in his eye and the younger made you an offer he didn't think you could refuse."

Pierre lifted his shoulders and let them drop. "What I figured was that neither one of them could afford to let me live. For Girard it was a matter of pride. And I knew what he was capable of. Years ago, he'd wanted to kill me for revenge because Marie and I had been lovers. He let me live for Marie, and now she had betrayed him by leaving me the necklace. I knew he would have his revenge this time. For Bernard, it was survival. For years LaBrecque International had been floundering under the mismanagement of his father. He had made plans for expansion, but he needed the money that the necklace would bring."

"So you agreed to steal the necklace?" Andrew asked.

"I agreed to go along with Bernard's plan because it bought me some time."

"You didn't think of going to the police?" Andrew asked.

Pierre shrugged. "I doubt they would have believed me. Even if they had, what would they have been able to do?"

Andrew sighed.

"I pretended to steal the necklace and replaced it with a fake because I wanted to give them enough rope to hang themselves. But I did not intend to involve Ms. Potter or put her in danger."

"How'd you manage the fake necklaces?" Andrew asked.

Pierre smiled. "I still have friends in the business."

"Why two?" Andrew asked.

"Because I suspected that Bernard would try to take it from me. I wanted to see what they would do once they found it was a fake."

"And none of that is going in the report," A.J. said. Then she turned to Pierre. "Tell me about Marie."

"She was lovely and young, and very romantic," Pierre said. A.J. saw the look that she'd seen before fill his eyes—a mixture of happiness and sadness.

"She must have loved you a great deal to have married Girard to save your life."

"She loved me in her own way," Pierre said and then shrugged. "But she had been born and raised for the kind of life that Girard could give her. She was having second thoughts about leaving the country with me. Who knows? Saving my life might have given her the perfect opportunity to make the choice her family wanted her to make."

A.J. frowned. "Then why did she leave you the necklace?"

"Who knows? Perhaps, after forty years, she wondered what it might have been like if she had chosen differently."

A.J. considered the possibility while Pierre and Andrew went over his statement again. But her mind was only half on the Marie-Girard-Pierre love triangle. Now that everything was winding down, she was going to have to do something about Sam.

"A.J., I'd like a word with you."

Turning, she saw her uncle and Rodney striding across the room toward her.

Sam stepped into Jamison Potter's path. "She's busy right now."

Her uncle glanced past Sam to meet her eyes. "It will only take a moment."

She nodded, then turned back to Pierre. "Don't sign anything until I can read it."

"You can use the interrogation room," Andrew said.

A.J. felt her headache growing steadily as she led her uncle and her cousin into the room and closed the door. The moment it clicked shut, Rodney said, "I hope you're satisfied. Thanks to you, Hancock, Potter and King has lost two important clients in one day."

"Rodney," Jamison began.

"It's the truth, Father. The LaBrecques are in jail, thanks to A.J. And now Parker Ellis Chase is taking his business elsewhere because she doesn't work for us anymore. It's all her fault."

"That will be enough, Rodney."

A.J. stared at the two men. She had never heard her uncle raise his voice to his son. Rodney's expression told her he was shocked and angry.

"I want you to apologize to your cousin, and then wait for me outside."

For a minute Rodney stared at his father, a flush rising in

his face. A.J. was sure he would refuse. But at the last moment, he turned to her. "Please accept my apology." Then he turned and strode stiffly from the room.

After her cousin left, there was silence in the room. A.J. studied her uncle. He'd been very firm with Rodney, but now he looked...uncertain.

"I must offer my apologies also," Jamison finally said, "for what happened last night. Rodney was so eager to bring in the LaBrecques as clients. But I should have consulted you before I sent Rabaut's files back and told the LaBrecques we would take them on."

"Yes, you should have," A.J. said. "But it wouldn't have made any difference. I still would have insisted on keeping Pierre Rabaut."

Her uncle gave her a thin smile. "But perhaps I could have prevented your resignation." He cleared his throat. "Last night you were upset. An important career decision should never be made in the heat of the moment. I'd like you to come back to the firm."

A.J. stared at him.

"If you're worried about a conflict of interest because of Rabaut and the LaBrecques, don't be. I've referred them to a very good firm that specializes in criminal defense work. And if you're worried about your cousin trying to undermine you, I'll handle Rodney. I can also promise you that Hancock, Potter and King will be referring more court cases your way."

He was offering her everything she'd wanted when she'd worn the skirt that first day. She glanced down at it in wonder.

"You don't have to answer me right now. I just want you to agree to think about it."

A.J. glanced up at him. "I guess I can agree to do that."

Her uncle gave her a brief nod before he moved toward

the door. With his hand on the knob, he turned back. "You'll be hearing from Parker Chase. He's very pleased with what you did for his son. Seems the boy is settling in at that place you sent him to. I wouldn't be surprised if you hear from Kirby and Caswell also. Chase told me that he was taking his business there on the condition that they offer you a job on the fast track to a partnership." Jamison met her eyes steadily. "I'll see that Hancock, Potter and King matches whatever they offer you."

After her uncle left, A.J. simply stared at the closed door for several seconds. Then it opened and Sam stepped into the room.

"Are you all right?" he asked.

"He just offered me my job back—and a fast track to a partnership," she said in a daze.

"Congratulations," he said stiffly. "It's what you wanted, isn't it?"

It had been, A.J. thought as she studied him. His hair was mussed. There were streaks of dirt on his clothes and his face. A slight scowl furrowed his brow. He looked tough and a little dangerous, much as he had those first days when she'd believed he was one of New York's homeless. And she knew that becoming a partner in a law firm wasn't the only thing she wanted.

"You're angry with me," she said.

"Yes. No." He scowled and began to pace. "I'm more angry with myself."

"Why?"

"I never should have taken you into the park. I should have figured out what was really going on. If I hadn't been so blind..." He stopped, then turned and looked at her. He'd been blinded in a way since the first instant he'd seen her. "You're such a tiny little bit of a thing, and all I've been able to see is the way you launched yourself at Bernard. Twice. I knew you would both times, just the way you took off to save Pierre and the bearded man from the hit-and-run." He raised his hands, then dropped them to his sides. "And I couldn't do anything to stop you. I was lying there on the ground, and I felt you get up and start to move away. And I told you to stay at my side."

"I was just doing what they do on the cop shows. I knew he couldn't keep the gun aimed at both of us. Besides, I had to move to give the skirt a chance to work."

Sam glanced at it and nearly lost what wits he had left. She might as well not have been wearing it. "Pull it down."

"Oh!" She glanced down and gave it a good, hard tug. She could have sworn that she could feel the silky material heat in her hands.

"You need a keeper," Sam said.

She studied him for a moment. He was definitely angry. He was also everything she'd ever wanted. "Would you like to apply for the job?" She watched some of the anger drain away. "I would prefer the term partner though."

All he was doing was staring at her. As nerves knotted in her stomach, A.J. considered going into the stare-step-wiggle routine, but she really wanted to get this finished on her own.

"Partner?"

"Yes." She cleared her throat. "I think we worked well together as Watson and Holmes. So I was thinking we could make it...permanent."

The grin came then, fast and lethal. Her knees nearly buckled as he started toward her. "How permanent?"

"Twenty-four hours a day, seven days a week."

"For how many years?"

She nearly smiled back at him. "Forever."

He was close enough to touch her when he said, "Counselor, are you asking me to marry you?"

She drew in a deep breath and let it out. "Yes."

His grin widened. "I want you to give me two good reasons."

She held up a finger. "Number one, because we work well together."

"That's my A.J. talking."

"And two, because I love you."

He finally touched her, framing her face with his hands, "And that's my Arianna talking. And I love both of you."

"Forever," she said as his lips finally brushed against hers.

AND AS THEY WATCHED Sam and A.J. kiss through the one-way glass of the interrogation room, both Andrew and Pierre could swear that they saw the skirt glow.

Epilogue

ELBOW TO ELBOW with her roommates, Samantha, Claire and A.J. stared at the three black skirts spread out on the sofa. Only one of them had special powers. They just had to figure out which one.

Tomorrow their lease on the apartment was up, and they'd invited Josh, Mitch and Sam over to meet each other and have a drink. Josh, Claire's new man, was in the kitchen opening a bottle of wine. Mitch, Samantha's new beau, and Sam were on their way.

"The skirts all look identical to me," Samantha said.

"I'm sure I wore the real one to Petra's show at the gallery," Claire said, frowning at the three skirts. "I'm just not sure which one it is now."

A.J. was equally certain that she had worn the real one to Central Park a week ago. She'd definitely been wearing it in that interrogation room at the precinct when she'd proposed to Sam.

At least she was pretty sure it had been the real skirt. When Claire left to open the door for Mitch, she leaned over to finger the material of the one she was betting on. Then she frowned as she tested the other ones. They all felt the same. A sliver of panic worked its way up her spine.

"You're just in time to help us figure out which skirt is the real one," Claire said as she led Mitch into the room.

"Yes, it's absolutely crucial that we find the real one," A.J. said, tapping her foot.

"I'll say it is," Mitch said. "Because I've already seen the effect that skirt has on men and I don't want my woman attracting every guy in the metropolitan area."

"I second that," Josh said as he joined them and passed each of them a glass of wine.

A.J. glanced at her watch. If only Sam would get here. She was sure that he would be able to spot the real one.

"Maybe we should each try on a skirt," Samantha suggested, "and let the guys tell us which one is the real thing."

"That sounds simple enough," A.J. said. And it would be quicker than waiting for Sam to get here. Sweeping the skirts up in her arms, she headed down the hallway. "Let's go change."

As soon as they reached the bedroom, Samantha said, "Is everything all right between you and the cute detective?"

Startled, A.J. dropped the skirts on the bed and turned to her friend. "Everything's fine." She thought of the past week, the way the Romanos had welcomed her into their family, and the job offer she'd received from Kirby and Caswell, which she'd accepted. In addition to a fast track to a partnership, they'd also offered her a spot on the team that would be handling the Parker Ellis Chase file. And then there was Sam—she felt the warmth move through her and smiled slowly. "More than fine. Why?"

Samantha shrugged. "He's not here yet, and you said it was *crucial* that we find the real skirt."

"It is," A.J. said as she stepped out of her jeans and pulled on what she thought was the real one. "I promised to lend it to someone." She glanced at her watch. "And I need it in the next fifteen minutes."

"Who?" Samantha asked. "No, wait. Claire will want to hear this too." Sticking her head out the door, she called, "Claire, are you coming?" Then she quickly changed into a skirt.

"Sorry," Claire said, rushing into the room. Then she stopped and beamed a smile at them. "No, I'm not. Mitch delayed me to give me this."

A.J. and Samantha moved toward her to study the hand she'd extended. The ring was vintage, a marquise diamond exquisitely set in a platinum band.

"It's lovely," Samantha said.

They all exchanged hugs.

"Your ring is just one more reason why we have to find out which skirt is the real one," A.J. said, blinking the dampness out of her eyes.

As Claire pulled on the final skirt, she asked, "Is there a problem, A.J.?"

"No. Everything's fine with the cute detective," Samantha explained. "A.J. wants to lend the skirt to someone. She was about to tell me who."

The two women turned toward A.J.

"Mrs. Higgenbotham."

"Mrs. H.?" Claire asked, staring.

"You're kidding," Samantha said.

"She's been dropping hints about it for the past week, ever since Franco told her that's how Cleo got Antoine," A.J. explained.

"Wait. Time out," Samantha said. "How did Franco figure that?"

"We each walked Cleo while we were wearing the skirt. He figures that when Cleo rubbed up against us, some of the skirt's magic rubbed off on her."

"And now Mrs. H. wants some of the magic too," Claire said. "Does she have someone special in mind?"

"Oh, yes. Sam's godfather, the retired jewel thief," A.J. muttered. "She's had her sights set on him ever since she first heard about him. So far they've only talked on the phone. But tonight he's invited her to his jazz club. It's their first date, and she begged me to let her borrow the skirt. Sam and I are going to be there, and Franco too. He's decided to write a screenplay about the adventures of the man-magnet skirt. And he wants to know if he can borrow it after Mrs. H. is through with it. He wants to use it for research."

"Mrs. H." Amused, Samantha shook her head. "Who would have thought the old gal had it in her?"

"Mrs. Higgenbotham and a retired jewel thief," mused Claire. "It just might work out."

The three of them turned to study themselves in the full-length mirror.

"It all worked out for us. We each found our true loves," A.J. said, taking Claire's hand as Claire took Samantha's. "I think it's time we passed the magic on."

"Just as soon as our true loves tell us which skirt has the magic," Samantha said as they moved into the hallway.

When they stepped into the living room, A.J.'s gaze went immediately to Sam. He was seated on the couch with Josh and Mitch.

"Well, which one of us is wearing the real skirt?" A.J. asked.

For a moment none of the men said a word. Then Sam rose and moved toward her. "You are, and I don't think you have any reason to wear that thing anymore."

A.J. looked past Sam to the other two men. "Do you two agree with him?"

"Yeah," Mitch said. "I don't recall that it ever looked quite that short on Claire."

A.J. glanced down to see that the skirt had hiked up while she was walking. Hurriedly, she tugged it down. "We have to be very certain."

Josh cleared his throat. "Even when you pull it down...the real one is very...revealing."

"That makes it unanimous," Samantha said as she sat down next to Josh.

"And that means you're changing out of it right now," Sam said with a glance at his watch. "We have ten minutes to deliver it to Mrs. Higgenbotham and get her to the club."

"You're giving the skirt to Mrs. Higgenbotham?" Josh asked.

A.J. glanced at her roommates and then back to Sam. "She wants to find her true love just as we did."

"Amen to that," Sam said as he raised his glass in a toast. When the others had raised their glasses too, he touched his to A.J.'s. "Here's to finding your true love."

* * * * *